Echoes of Camusfearna

Copyright © Paul and Grace Yoxon 1997

First published 1997

ISBN 1 899171 76 2

British Library Cataloguing-in-Publication Data.
A catalogue record for this book is available from the British Library.

Cover design and book layout by David Gregson.
Central cover photo by Emil Barbelette.
Printed and bound by Interprint Ltd., Malta

Acknowledgements
Ring of Bright Water © Gavin Maxwell Enterprises 1960,
Raven Seek Thy Brother © Gavin Maxwell Enterprises 1968 and *The Watcher at the Door* © Gavin Maxwell Enterprises 1951.
Ring of Bright Water is published by Penguin Books.

Published by
Findhorn Press
The Park, Findhorn, Forres IV36 0TZ, Scotland
tel +44 (0)1309 690582 • fax 690036
email thierry@findhorn.org
http://www.gaia.org/findhornpress/

Echoes of Camusfearna

by Paul and Grace Yoxon

FINDHORN Press

Contents

To Kirsty, Ben and Connaire

THE WATCHER AT THE DOOR

ALL THROUGH THE NIGHT I WATCHED THE RUINED DOOR,
INTENT, AS GAMBLERS WATCH THE FALL OF DICE;
AWAITING VERDICT, PRISONER AT THE BAR.
SHADOWS CROSSED IT, ONCE I HEARD A VOICE.

AT DAWN A MOUNTAIN HIND EMERGED ALONE,
QUICK STEP AND SURE AS WITH SOME PURPOSE KNOWN,
SOME WILL THAT ANIMATED THE UNMARROWED BONE,
FOR THROUGH HER RIBS I SAW THE LICHENED STONE.

AT NOON A NAKED FORM WAS THERE;
A WATCHER, INDISTINCT, BEGAN
TO FOLLOW AS IT TURNED AND RAN
SEAWARD OVER THE SHORE.

AT DUSK A BROKEN WHEEL APPEARED
HELD BY A HAND I COULD NOT SEE,
AND I KNEW THAT SOMEONE WHOM I FEARED
HAD DISCOVERED AN EMPTY ROOM IN ME.

—Gavin Maxwell (1951)
from *Gavin Maxwell – A Life*, by Douglas Botting (HarperCollins)

Introduction

"I sit in a pitch-pine panelled Kitchen-Living room, with an otter asleep upon its back among the cushions on the sofa." It must be about 20 years now since I first read these opening words of Gavin Maxwell's wonderful book *Ring of Bright Water,* which described his loves and losses, trials and tribulations with the wildlife of the Hebrides. It is difficult to say whether it was this book which influenced Grace and me to want to live on the Hebridean Island of Skye so many years later but we had a dream to come here and make Skye and its wildlife our home and our work. But in living here and trying to help wildlife, we found time and time again that the reality of progress seems to lie on a collision course with the natural environment.

We started the Skye Field Centre (now the Skye Environmental Centre) in 1984 and at that time our idea was to use the house as a guest house and take people for walks to see the geology, archaeology and wildlife. Little did we know how this would evolve and the concept we had in our heads then was totally different to what we are doing today; in fact, it could be said that on that cold December day in 1984 we were trying to break away from the rat race, to live where animals and humans are in harmony; but soon we found that even on Skye nothing could be further from the truth.

Our experience has been that as we come closer to nature, we come closer to ourselves and we are then driven with an ever-increasing fire to protect it and do something positive to preserve this wonderful environment.

We began by organising a whole spectrum of special interest holidays for groups or individuals who would join us for the week. Sometimes we would have a school, sometimes

a natural history club or sometimes a mixture of people from all over the world and of all different ages and backgrounds. There was no "standard" group. Still today we take visitors to some of the most beautiful islands in Britain watching otters, seals, eagles, whales and dolphins, and over the last four years we have expanded our range and now take groups into the Taiga Forest of Russia.

But our work now is so much more than this: the Skye Environmental Centre grew out of the Field Centre, providing a source of information for visitors and local people on various aspects of the natural environment of the area; the hospital developed naturally as people started to bring us injured birds and animals because they knew we cared about wildlife; we now treat about 200 casualties a year, including seals, otters, owls, sparrowhawks, gulls, hedgehogs and mice. But equally important is the fact that other people are starting to care too: children come running down carrying a small bird they have found unconcious by the roadside; local people are telling us about their wonderful experiences watching an otter on the shore by their house; visitors are seeing what a treasure we have here and how important it is to look after it and hopefully they will take some of this home and look around for their own local treasures.

People join us from the whole spectrum of humanity; some have visited many lands and cultures and may now be exploring some of the more remote parts of their own country; some are fascinated particularly by birds, some by flowers, some by otters; some love walking anywhere that is quiet and peaceful; and some have never done much walking, know nothing about wildlife and have never visited Scotland. But it really does not matter at all, as the only thing that is truly vital is an open interest and willingness to look, feel and enjoy – that is all. Everyone has not only something to learn but something to contribute. It is frustrating at times when someone says "but I know nothing"; maybe they do not know how to identify flowers or birds, or when the Iron Age was, but often these people, uncluttered by so-called academic knowledge, have a deep love and caring which is contagious. If only some of this rubs off on other members of the party, they have made the most valuable contribution of all.

So many of our guests are now good friends and return year after year and it is impossible to include a mention of everyone. Equally it is impossible to tell every happy, sad, comical, strange or inspiring story. So we have just taken a selection of events and places, and hope that those of you who were with us will recall the pleasure and peace of these mainly happy times together and that those of you whom we do not know can, through this book, share these experiences with us and feel something of the inspiration of the Hebrides.

As you read on, we would like to share with you our vision of living with nature – the vision which sometimes seemed tarnished and sometimes shattered but which was always our driving force. Whether we fulfil it only time will ever tell, but it is a fact that if we humans are going to survive on this planet, it can only be achieved by living in balance with our natural environment and not, as we are continually doing, by pulling against it.

Some may think it idealistic that one small concern on a small island hundreds of miles away from Whitehall can hope to achieve anything, but each small link becomes a chain which cannot be broken.

Today, our home on the Island of Skye is also the headquarters for the International Otter Survival Fund (IOSF), which we set up in 1993, dedicated to helping all thirteen species of the world's otters. We believe a world without these furry, aquatic mammals is a sad world, as is a world without clear coastal waters, without clean river systems, lakes and estuaries. IOSF is today working with people worldwide, identifying threats to otters and taking steps to overcome these, thus preserving habitats not just for otters but for all wildlife and ultimately for ourselves. To date, IOSF has set up the first otter rehabilitation centre in the Highlands and Islands of Scotland, where we care for sick and orphaned otters until they are ready to return to the wild; we have funded research in Turkey and Russia, set up a local branch of IOSF in the Ukraine, and assisted in many projects from Chile to Portugal; and our latest project is working with Wetlands International on a programme in Indonesia to conserve four species of otter.

I may not be in a pitch-pine panelled kitchen/living room, more like a modern office with computer, fax machine and photocopier, but as I write I have an eleven-week old otter cub asleep on my lap.

Chapter 1 ~ Paul

"AFOOT AND LIGHT HEARTED I TAKE TO THE OPEN ROAD, HEALTHY, FREE AND THE WORLD BEFORE ME,
THE LONG BROWN PATH BEFORE ME LEADING WHEREVER I CHOOSE"

—WALT WHITMAN

'Soon be Christmas, Grace", I said, as I leaned over to see her dozing on the back seat of the Landrover. It was really snowing hard now, and the darkness crept in and blanketed the surrounding hillside. Lights flickered as the snow fell on the deserted road. It wouldn't be long before we reached the ferry – maybe an hour if we kept up this speed. Well, 30 miles an hour is fast for a Landrover which is so heavily laden. It seemed a long time since we left Perthshire on that beautiful winter's afternoon in 1984, with every last possession in the whole world in or tied to this Landrover. We had to reach the ferry before it stopped for Christmas. Behind me sat Grace and six-month-old Kirsty half sharing a seat with a frying pan and a rather frisky Border collie, surrounded by everything we owned in the world.

The Landrover chugged on up a hill with the black road becoming whiter by the minute. This was our second attempt to settle and live on Skye. One and a half years ago, we had rented a little croft house in Lower Breakish. I had spent half my life on the oil rigs and the other half on Skye, but the constant travelling soon became too tiring and we moved to Perthshire to a land-based job.

Our plan as we returned was to set up a field centre in a converted guest house on the outskirts of Broadford. The idea of a field centre on Skye was not new – it had been talked about for years but in the end nothing had ever become of it.

It is funny how ideas come to you – they come with a flash of inspiration, often from a chance remark – and the idea of the Skye Field Centre was no exception. I can remember sitting in our house in Comrie in Perthshire. The job which had taken us away from Skye had ended quite suddenly and I had been unemployed for nearly a year. I was writing letters constantly, but as anyone who has been in this sort of situation knows, the replies are always disappointing. However, the letter in front of me was different. It was from someone who ran another field centre and, true, he also said he could not help, but he went one step further – had we thought of starting a field centre on Skye? Yes, of course, we had thought of running a field centre on Skye, but it had not occurred to us that *we* could actually start it. The more we thought about it, the more the idea grew until we decided that we actually could make it a reality.

Now, obviously, we believed in the idea, but it was a different matter to convince someone to lend us the money to get a centre going, especially when I was unemployed and we were expecting a baby.

Finding the initial finance for our business was one of the greatest problems we had to overcome and to anyone in a similar situation my advice is to never take no for an answer. It took us 29 attempts until finally the Clydesdale Bank liked our idea and gave us the loan to buy the property and the initial start to succeed.

Our journey continued as I pondered on what had already happened and what lay ahead. The snow lay thicker on the road as we passed the Cluanie Inn with its dim lights shining through the storm. It was not long before Shiel Bridge came into view; the houses sat comfortably lit and plumes of smoke rose into the white sky. You could picture the people nice and cosy in front of their warm, glowing fires.

We now had only about 16 miles to go and the Landrover chugged its way along the windy road and soon we reached Balmacara and eventually Kyle of Lochalsh. At Kyle the snow had turned to sleet and it lashed against the sides of the Landrover. Drip, drip, came the water through both doors, making pools on the floor and soaking into the newly fitted carpet. The ferry was on the Skye side and we sat all alone on the jetty at Kyle awaiting its return.

It arrived 15 minutes later and we drove on. No one else was crossing at that time and so the ferry left for the five minute journey to arrive at Kyleakin on the Isle of Skye. We looked at each other as we approached the slip. This time we were going to stay. We could not leave Skye a second time.

Our new home was to be a guest house in Harapool with the capacity to take 14 people. It was only eight miles from Kyleakin and soon we stood in anticipation on the doorstep. The sleet had stopped now and the sky had cleared to reveal a million stars that glistened and twinkled. We unlocked the door and stepped in. The place was empty; every room was bare and light-bulbs hung from the ceilings, throwing a harsh glare onto the bare walls and wooden floors. We had three months until we opened, £3000 in the bank and a headful of ideas. The door slammed shut and the adventure began.

Chapter 2 ~ Paul

"TO SAY WE LOVE GOD AND AT THE SAME TIME EXERCISE CRUELY TOWARD THE LEAST CREATURE MOVING BY HIS LIFE OR BY LIFE DERIVED FROM HIM WAS A CONTRADICTION IN ITSELF"

—JOHN WOOLMAN

The next day was Christmas. Outside a thick frost had turned all the grass white and frozen the pools of seawater on the shore. Near the high-tide mark the seaweed had frozen into contorted patterns looking like a landscape from some far-off planet. In the distance birds of various kinds fed amongst the rocks and seaweed of the water-line – oystercatchers, turnstones and curlew, together with a selection of gulls.

Our house had been carefully chosen and every bedroom had wonderful views out over the bay. The rooms were comfortable with wash basins and heating, and rather than using large dormitories, which is becoming a thing of the past, we could provide single, double and twin bedrooms. The house lay only 30 feet from high water. It was a dream about to come true, but first we had the hard work, and we spent the morning tidying and cleaning.

After a snack lunch, we walked out along the shore towards the township of Waterloo. The sun shone strongly and was extremely warm, considering the ground was still frozen. High above we could see the typical V-shape of a skein of Greenland white fronted geese which winter around Skye. We headed for Ardnish and watched two harbour seals bobbing in the clear blue water, and if you could picture seals smiling, these two certainly were. They dived and re-emerged and for most of the afternoon we watched them and, like all curious animals, they watched us.

It was lovely not only to see but also to hear the variety of birds which littered the shoreline: the bubbling curlew gave out a whirl of noise; the frequent peeping of the oystercatcher and the rasp of herons made the music of the shoreline.

By now the sun was setting behind the granite dome of Beinn na Caillich and as it slid slowly down, the air temperature chilled by the second. Two grey herons flew past, heading for their roosts, as the light faded rapidly. It was time for us to leave too, and we quickly retraced our steps back to the house.

We spent our first evening back on Skye having a delicious Christmas dinner with some friends and although it was different to the usual celebrations, I think this is probably one of the best Christmases I can remember.

Over the next three months our spare time was very limited as we had to decorate, to re-wire, to paint outside and inside, to re-carpet and carry out countless other jobs. Our rather outdated central heating boiler had not been used for some time and was in major need of overhaul, which was obviously a priority in view of the temperature.

The time was full of incidents – some funny and some not so funny, although looking back we can now laugh at more of them than we did at the time. We had numerous burst pipes as the winter of 1984 took its toll and if I can just recapture one occasion you will get the idea.

We had been away for the weekend during February. It was still cold and frosty and as our old diesel Landrover would not start in these extreme conditions, we had decided to take the train. On our return, the Skye landscape looked like the Arctic: the mountains and moors were white and frost gripped every inch of the bare silver birch trees which grew in clumps on the roadside. We took the bus back to Broadford and in the driveway stood our Landrover encased in ice, like some tomb of the ice-god. We entered the house and I turned on the water – nothing happened. I fiddled about for about an hour but still no water. This was serious – without water no heating, no coffee, no flush toilet; it is quite incredible how dependent we are on this rather common luxury item.

We spent that night without water and in the morning I phoned the Water Board. Graham was very prompt. He came round and checked the house supply and then concluded that the fault must be at the road, where our own supply joined the general pipe.

"Who put this pipe in? " he yelled. "Not me", I quickly replied, as he went on, "It should have been buried much deeper. It's far too shallow; the frost can easily freeze it."

After much digging and thinking, the pipe was finally exposed and a blowlamp was run over it. "Let's try it now", Graham said, and the stopcock at the road was re-opened allowing the water to gush forward at great speed.

The torrent rushed through the top field, under the garden, under the driveway and then flooded into our newly decorated house. It entered our pipes and rushed easily along them as it made its way to the immersion heater. Then, oh yes, then it reached the joint; the joint which broke and allowed a cascade of gallons of water on to the ceiling, causing it to buckle and collapse onto the new carpet.

"Turn it off, turn it off", I screamed. "There's a leak."

Eventually, after what seemed like an eternity, the water slowly stopped and we sat down to cry over the situation. They say you should never cry over spilled milk, but spilled water is a completely different matter.

Mind you, it was not long before things were put right. By the only stroke of luck, the room which was flooded was for our own personal use rather than for guests; but even today this room, which is now occupied by our eight-year-old daughter, still has a bowed ceiling which serves as a constant reminder of our early days.

We had many more such "watery" occasions before our first groups started to arrive, and although rather painful at the time, looking back on them can and often does make us laugh. We worked so hard throughout the winter of 1984 that we were not able to enjoy much of it, but we had to be ready to start our trips.

Taking groups of people out on excursions is no easy task; we learnt to cultivate a mind and memory which can regurgitate facts and figures about all sorts of things. What is that flower? What is the name of that little bird with the flash on its wing? Can you name this rock? As the years progressed we have learnt a lot about wildlife and natural history from being out in the field and observing things as they really are rather than as they appear in books. This is by far the best way to learn. Sure, books play a part but they cannot be any substitute for the real thing. But even today you will still find book naturalists spouting off like experts while never moving from the comforts of their own library and seeing for themselves what actually does happen.

In the early days, we really didn't know what to expect of our first guests. We just assumed everyone would be different, and we waited patiently, if a little apprehensively, for them to arrive.

In the years to follow, having come in contact with so many different kinds of people, I have eventually learnt that really people are generally similar can quite easily be grouped on either side of an imaginary green fence. On one side are the monetaristic materialistic people who are self-centred and care only for themselves, and on the other are the caring, considerate, sharing people who show many tinges of green from pale to bottle. What is evident in people who have a true interest in wildlife is their total dedication to all living things and their appreciation that they are all a part of a complicated web of life.

We are fortunate to have on our courses mostly caring people with a wide range of interests covering the whole spectrum of the natural and physical sciences. Our initial apprehensions were therefore unfounded and our very first course got off to a good start.

It was Sunday. The sky was crystal-clear and a cold breeze swept in from the sea as we set off on our first expedition with our faithful friend, the Landrover, whisking us away through Broadford and beyond. Our plan was to head for Suishnish and Boreraig, two cleared villages along the Strathaird peninsula.

As we passed Loch Cill Christ two whooper swans lifted into the air and made their way over Beinn Dearg Beag. These swans are winter visitors to Skye and in the dreary winter months small groups of them can be seen on some of the inland lochs. Unlike the more familiar mute swans found in so many parks, the whoopers are noisy birds with a loud trumpeting call. They can also be distinguished at a distance because they hold their head and neck straight and have a yellow rather than orange beak.

The two birds of Cill Christ took to flight and we watched them with their slow powerful wingbeats as they disappeared over the hillside. Very soon they would be flying back to the Arctic tundra only to return in October to spend the winter in our relatively less hostile environment.

We continued on our journey and on reaching Camas Malag, the view across to Eigg and Rhum – those small isles set afloat on the waters of the Little Minch – was breathtaking. To our right towered Blaven and the Clach Glas ridge with the white cottages of Faoilean nestling below.

From here our road took a turn for the worse and deteriorated into a rough track which was extremely bumpy but exhilarating. Overhead flew a pair of buzzards calling to one another and below the sea was calm and flat as the proverbial millpond. The track went on for three miles and we stopped in the township which was once Suishnish, with its tumbled down crofts – a ruinous memorial to the Highland Clearances. From there we took the coastal path to Boreraig, another cleared village.

The whole history of the Clearances has been suppressed by many of the English historians and until recently was little taught in Scottish schools. It was fuelled by some of the greedy lairds who owned so much of the Highland land. These lairds gave the people small areas of ground called crofts in which they tried to scrape a living, but the ground was definitely not sufficient, so the crofters had to work for the lairds in return for very little money. They collected seaweed which was used by the chemical industry but when modern chemicals became available the bottom dropped out of the market and the people became surplus to requirements. The lairds moved into sheep farming and therefore had no further use for the people – so they evicted them.

Suishnish and Boreraig are just two townships on Skye which were cleared in the mid-1800s but this was happening on a massive scale throughout the whole Highland area.

Picture the scene. It is January 1854 and the people of Boreraig are busy at their work. In April 1853 many of the people had been offered a choice of assisted passage to Australia or movement to another part of the estate. Some had taken up either option but many people had stayed.

All in all, 150 people in 32 families remained, trying to scrape a living from the soil. A snowstorm had started and not far away the Macdonald estate officers were making their way over the hill to evict the people.

On their arrival they quickly set to their task, pulling out the furniture and later burning the houses. Some of the people were over 80 years old and one, Flora Robertson, was a widow aged 96. People with small children were driven out into the snow and old Flora was dragged out of her son's house. She was assisted to a neighbouring sheep shelter by two of her grandchildren, but it was a cold and damp place, and as the old lady lay on the damp straw her face and arms had the colour of lead. Flora died over the winter. Another man perished in the night through exposure and cold, having returned from the hills to find his house in ruins. By spring 1854 the township was empty and the area was dead.

As we stared at the remains of the croft walls on this bright spring day, sheep grazed all over the crofting area, skylarks sang and darted above the first spring flowers, and high above the granite crags of Carn Dearg a solitary golden eagle soared on the thermals. The setting was wonderful and yet the land here was sad. It cried at the cruelty of man.

Chapter 3 ~ Grace

"CLIMB THE MOUNTAINS AND GET THEIR GOOD TIDINGS. NATURE'S PEACE WILL FLOW INTO YOU AS SUNSHINE FLOWS INTO TREES. THE WINDS WILL BLOW THEIR OWN FRESHNESS INTO YOU, AND THE STORMS THEIR ENERGY, WHILE CARES WILL DROP OFF LIKE AUTUMN LEAVES."

—JOHN MUIR

The cruelty of some human beings seems to know no limits, not only to their own species but to all creatures with which they come into contact. The history of wildlife is a catalogue of human destructiveness: at one time Scotland boasted wolves, bears, elk, beavers, sea eagles, but now of these only the sea eagle remains, and that is only because it was re-introduced. And on Skye, not only is this cruelty to other human beings, as shown by the Clearances, but it has been and still is inflicted on our own native wildlife.

The last native sea eagle was shot at Rudh an Dunain on Skye in 1916; wolves once roamed our island too as witnessed by the wolf pits in the north west; and wildcats also seem to have been present as there are several place names which include the word "cat". One such is Coire-chat-achan just outside Broadford, where Boswell and Dr Johnson stayed during their travels to the west coast.

But although we have lost these species, we still have a great variety of wildlife within such a small area – otters, deer (red and roe), foxes, eagles, peregrines, sparrowhawks, merlins, ring ouzels, corncrakes, divers, and around our shores you will find common and grey seals, whales, dolphins and porpoises. What other island can boast all these and much more?

It is sometimes said that Skye is not good for birds. This is true compared to Shetland and Orkney, where there are massive seabird cliff colonies, but I always defend the island.

After all, it is easy to spot a gannet amongst a thousand of them, although the scale of such vast colonies is impressive; Skye just makes you work harder for your birds. But it provides such great rewards with far more variety (over 150 species have been recorded) and unforgettable experiences – eagles soaring over high cliffs and being mobbed by hooded crows, the haunting call of the ring ouzel within the eerie landscape of the Storr, and the comical coo-ing of the eider ducks.

Skye is really an island of extremes: there are 1000 miles of coastline with high cliffs, rocky shores, small sandy beaches – including the black sands of Talisker – and salt marsh. Within this we have the highest mountain range of any island in Britain with the rugged Cuillin peaks rising sheer from the sea contrasting with the gentler rounded Red Hills; heather moorlands cover the vast lava flows of the northern part of the island and small pockets of native woodland cling to more sheltered areas as in Sleat. For those who know Skye, these are all familiar images, but for those who do not, they cannot begin to conjure up the full beauty of the island.

However, Skye is famed for its weather and I know it is an old cliché but it is true that if we had a penny for every time someone says "it always rains on Skye", I am sure we would be millionaires by now. To be honest, it gets pretty boring assuring people that even though it happens to have poured for the whole of their two-week holiday, we do have periods of unbelievable hot and sunny weather. Of course, they never believe us, but that is fine, because otherwise we would be over-run with people, as on the Costa del Sol. Paul often says that Skye's biggest assets are the weather and the midge: it means that the visitors who do come have to be something special because these two factors frighten away many less discerning tourists.

One thing is certain – when the weather is fine there is no more beautiful part of the world, but when it is bad it can be absolutely foul. There is no pussy-footing around when it rains, because it is usually accompanied by a howling gale and no matter how good your waterproofs are the rain will find some small gap to penetrate and soak you.

Skye weather is varied and totally unpredictable. One day it will be lashing rain and gales and the next it will be like a millpond with clear blue skies – you can never call it boring. And you must always be prepared for it to change in an instant as you can virtually have all four seasons in one day – so we never ever go anywhere without waterproofs.

Skye is also famed as the "island of mist" but we do not often get fog. Many times we see on the weather forecast that other areas have thick fog but it is rare here. We do have sea mists and the hills may be covered in cloud, so maybe this is how the name arose.

But in the hills in particular these mists can be literally lethal: one minute you can see the whole ridge clearly outstretched before you and the next you can barely see a few feet in front. Normally in these circumstances you would resort to using your compass, but the Cuillins have the added danger of being composed of a rock so full of iron that it disturbs compasses and gives totally false readings. Really then the only way is by knowing the area, but sometimes even those who know the hills well can lose their way. A friend of ours, for example, had decided to go up Blaven one promising day. She had been up several times before and was quite familiar with the route. However, once she and her companion reached the top the mist suddenly came down. They waited for a while to see if it would lift but then decided to head down, as they knew which way to go. There are several deep and dangerous gullies on Blaven and they knew they had to keep to the right of these, but when they dropped below the mist they found that they had gone too far to the right and were now well on the way to Camusunary. On this occasion they were lucky – all it meant was that they had a much longer walk back than they had expected – but it serves as a great warning. They knew the dangers and the route, yet even then they went wrong. How would it have been for someone climbing the mountain for the first time not knowing the various pitfalls?

In the early part of the year the scenery can be stunning with the snow-covered Cuillin peaks slicing their icy way through clear skies. February days can sometimes be pure "Christmas card" and even the wildlife seems to appreciate the break in the winter grey and the lengthening days: eagles are establishing their pair bonds with fantastic aerial displays of soaring glides and dramatic sky-dives and otters reveal their more mischievous and playful character as they romp and slide through the snow. February may also see the first alpine flowers as the buds of purple saxifrage begin to push their way upward through the snow.

Sometimes temperatures drop to a vicious −15°C and yet other times it can be so mild that you end up working outside in short sleeves while the rest of the country shivers. We have even seen tulips out in the garden in February, although it is hard to believe. For two years the winters were extremely mild but horrendous with continual rain for almost three months. Although you get used to quite a bit of rain, it does begin to get you down after so long and everywhere was just a quagmire.

February, then, proves how variable our weather can be, so imagine how we reacted one February morning when a young man came in and asked "Can you tell me what the weather is going to do for the next week or so?" "You see," he went on "the forecast said snow and as I am going to camp in the hills I want to know how long I am going to be snowed in." If I had been able to predict the weather like that, I would have made my fortune long ago.

It is often said that otters prefer good weather, but is it not the otter-watcher who likes good weather? After all, if it is a nice day you are more likely to have patience and sit and wait, and so you are more likely to be rewarded with a sighting of an otter than on a grotty day when you stick your head out of the car and say "no otters here today".

On one typical cold, showery, windy winter's day we went down to the Otter Hide at Kylerhea. We had our lunch with us and a flask and were quite happy to spend some time there. We watched the seals for a while and then, after about half an hour Paul spotted a female otter with her cub. She came in from our right until she reached the stream which flows into the sea just below the hide and there she set to fishing. She caught several fish while the cub played around in the shallows and brought them ashore where they shared the meal. The weather had begun to deteriorate: the rain had turned to snow and the showers were now becoming more solid. It was time to go, as the road to Kylerhea is not really one to travel in heavy snow unless you have to. One last look at the otter and her young one; they were totally unperturbed by the near blizzard conditions and continued to fish and play in what to us would have been unbearably cold water. So much for otters liking good weather...

As the days lengthen further, more spring flowers begin to appear – primroses, violets, lesser celandine and later marsh marigold and the beautiful early purple orchid. April also sees the arrival of wheatears with their cheeky white flash above the tail. The geese, whooper swans and wigeons have normally left by the end of April, but it is always hard to say exactly when they have all gone. (It is much more noticeable when you spot the first migrants arrive but you only realise they have gone some time after their actual departure.)

I think, if I have to pick a favourite month it must be May – of course I was born in May, but that is a bonus. May is the best month for flowers, birds are nesting and many summer visitors (feathered) are already here. There are the typical spring flowers: primroses, violets and bluebells – the blue and white carpet of bluebells and wild garlic on the way up to the house of Tigh Ard on the Isle of Canna must be one of the simplest and yet most beautiful woodland sights I know. Another May flower is mountain avens, a very selective plant which only grows on lime-rich rocks and which has the amazing ability to track the sun, so that the centre of the flower is slightly warmer and so attracts insects for pollination. On the Trotternish ridge, May is also the best month for alpine flowers with moss campion, mossy cyphel, mossy saxifrage, roseroot and amongst the rocky pillars the clear call of ring ouzels.

Generally our weather is best in this early part of the year, particularly April, May and June, and then as soon as the school holidays start the heavens open. Most people therefore assume that this means they will see nothing in terms of wildlife. How wrong they can be.

On one occasion, I was to lead a group and it was one of those days of constant torrential rain. However, we decided to go anyway and it was heads down and into the wind. We definitely won't see anything today, I thought to myself. But as we dropped down the hillside I glanced up to see a golden eagle battling against the wind. The power of the bird against the gale was incredible as it fought its way forward. I wouldn't have thought it would find much in the way of prey but it obviously felt the effort worthwhile.

Animals and birds have to eat regardless of the weather and although they would prefer to hunt in good conditions, if they are hungry they have to just put up with it. They do not have the option of seeing what they have in the freezer.

The advantage of botany and geology is that the rocks and plants are still there regardless of the weather, although of course sometimes flowering can be late or early. The main summer flowers of Skye are orchids and the moorlands are strewn with spotted orchids, both common and heath, interspersed with such orchid gems as butterfly, fragrant, pyramidal, marsh and frog.

But do not be fooled into thinking that our summers are always wet and windy: we can have really hot summers and people can never believe that from time to time we are even threatened with drought. One July we had a school group from Yorkshire and they had been well and truly warned about our awful weather. They came armed with woolly jumpers and waterproofs, but what they did not expect was a heatwave. In fact, that particular week it was announced on the television that the area of the Hebrides was the hottest place in Europe. By the end of the week there was not a pair of jeans left intact – they had all been cut down to shorts in desperation, and every day we had to ensure lunch was by water so that everyone could have a swim to cool off. Unfortunately, the students would not cover up under the powerful sun and so we had a few nasty cases of sunburn.

The summer also sees the arrival of the common seal pups. These pups are not the typical white-coated pup so often seen in pictures, although they are still very endearing. They do have a white coat but this is shed while they are still in their mother's womb and so when they are born they are just tiny replicas of the adults. They weigh only 10 kg at birth and yet swim straight away. They really have no choice as they are born on a typical haul-out site of tidal rocks and so when the tide comes, they just have to follow Mum. The bond between mother and pup seems to be quite close in common seals and often you see them swimming together or even the Mum giving her baby a "piggy-back".

Other babies are also appearing. Eagle chicks are on the nest and ducklings of eider, merganser and shelduck are seen scooting about on the water. But other creatures are also emerging which are not nearly as popular – the midge. These infamous beasties spoil many a beautiful sunset. You know the scene: it is a lovely evening and the sea lies still and calm beneath the reddening sky. You sit on a rock to watch the gentle lapping of the water and then it starts – tickle, bite, scratch, tickle, bite, scratch – followed by a few choice words and a rapid retreat indoors. Of course, there are various creams, lotions and even a sonic repellent, but to be honest none of them are the wonder-cure their manufacturers profess them to be.

Yes, the midge really can turn a camping holiday into a nightmare and we all long for the heroic scientist who develops the magic solution to get rid of the midge for ever. Or do we? Let's remove the midge and get an idea of what the real effect will be. Do we know how many other species are dependent on these horrors for food? We would lose our insectivorous plants – the beautiful and delicate sundews and the purple-flowered butterwort. What about the insect-eating birds such as swallows? Then there are bats – it is said that an average pipistrelle bat, although tiny, can eat 3000 midges in an average night's feeding. Yes, removing midges may seem idyllic, but we would lose so much more than the urge to scratch!

There have also been suggestions of using biological controls such as parasites which are specific only to the midge. Again this seems to be the answer, but we must be very wary as sometimes species are found to have a much wider taste in new environments than in their natural habitat simply because the choice was not available to them before, and so the problem increases.

This happens all too often with our so called solutions. We think we are so clever but we look at things so narrowly that we do not see the overall picture. How many times have we thought that we have solved a problem only to find that we have created a greater one? How many times have species been introduced to deal with a pest only to spread so rapidly that it too becomes a pest? Nature has food chains so precisely arranged that we cannot really comprehend their intricacies and our meddling only upsets the balance.

So yes, let's develop an effective repellent, but let's not look into sprays, chemicals and biological introductions to irradicate the midge for ever.

Late in summer the hills turn their traditional purple colour as heather comes into flower and in the really wet areas you could look for that beautiful white prize, the Grass of Parnassus, which is found in late August and September. Otherwise this is not a particularly good time for flowers as the orchids and alpines are all more or less over.

However, the youngsters of the year are now getting more adventurous and getting ready to leave home. The eagle chicks are making their maiden flights and otter cubs are leaving the holt. Some people say that otters breed throughout the year and so you can see young cubs at any time of the year. This does not seem to be the case in Shetland where the cubs first leave the holt in late summer, and Skye, in general, seems to hold with Shetland, although out of season cubs are known.

And so to autumn. This is another lovely time of year as the trees turn to their beautiful colours. Although Skye is not renowned for its forests, the autumn colours are still breathtakingly beautiful particularly when the late afternoon sun sets fire to the bronzed bracken. September can be a lovely month and is another traditional time for visiting Scotland. At this time the red deer begin to gather for the annual rut and the migrating birds start to head south. Manx shearwaters are always a sign of September as they set off on their annual migration to South America. However, in bad weather young birds can become exhausted and confused; seeing the wet road beneath, they think this is water and land for a rest. These birds nest in hollows on hillsides and cannot actually take off from flat ground; so there on the road they stay to become prey either to a passing cat or car. Every September we have reports of these birds and fortunately all that needs to be done is to catch them, keep them quiet overnight and then release them over water in the morning.

October, too, can be lovely but it is starting to get cold and the air has a "wintry" feel to it. This is the time when grey seals gather on their traditional breeding grounds and the largest colonies in the world are to be found off the Western Isles. Grey seals are much larger than the common (up to 2 metres compared with 1.6 metres for the adult common seal) and they are generally a much "wilder" animal, preferring the rugged uninhabited islands way out in the Atlantic. Each year, we visit one of these islands to see the grey seals and their pups, but more of this later.

Grey seal pups are white-coated, black-eyed beauties who simply beg to be loved. However, they are also armed with a fearsome set of teeth and even a young one can give a nasty bite. Unlike the commons, they do not go in the water for some time: their mother feeds them for up to three weeks until they resemble fat, hairy little barrels and then she leaves them to fend for themselves. They stay ashore until they have moulted the white coat and then they wander down to the water and start to learn to fish. The pups run into problems in their first few weeks of life during gales and high tides when they run the risk of being washed off the colony and separated from Mum and so if there is a period of bad weather, we hold our breath and wait for the phone call telling us of an abandoned pup.

Gales on the west coast can be tremendous. As with the rain, there is no messing about with a strong wind – the sheer strength of the wind can be frightening. I have been physically picked up and dumped in the middle of the road while I was walking along minding my own business. I have known caravans to be thrown over six-foot-high walls and a car was once blown off the pier at Sconser. These might be extremes, but every year there are terrific gales at some time and when they come it is a case of don't go anywhere unless you really have to.

Sometimes the gales occur at the back end of the year and sometimes early on in February, but come they will. At one time we had two fibreglass pools for seals, which were set in front of the house. It had been a real "howler" of a night and I got up in the morning and glanced out of the window. In my usual semi-conscious "first thing in the morning" state I could tell that something was different, but I could not make out what. Then I realised – where the seal pools had been was a big gaping hole where the winds had forced the tide upwards and washed away the pools. Fortunately no seals were using them at the time and we then set to replacing them with a stronger concrete pool to withstand the tidal battering.

October can have some lovely clear nights, though and at this time we are often fortunate to have fantastic display of the Northern Lights. The first time I saw them was actually on Harris, where they were like a lot of searchlights sweeping the night sky. Sometimes they are just a light glow in the sky, but if you are particularly lucky you can be treated to the most wonderful light show – pinks and greens shimmering and flickering with shafts of coloured light offshoots. Shooting stars are often also seen, so that the night sky becomes a light spectacle.

And into winter. The snow has arrived on the hills possibly as early as October and from August onwards, if the waters are calm, we are treated to the rising and falling fins of the local porpoises, who stay with us until about January. Sometimes people are disappointed not to see them – they are there but it needs still waters to spot them. They may come really close inshore when they are easily visible with the naked eye, but we have become spoilt with the images of leaping dolphins on television.

Whooper swans and Greenland white-fronted geese return in about October and redwings and fieldfares also trust us for their winter quarters. Birds and animals are starting to find it more difficult to find food and it is up to us to help them out where we can.

Sometimes though they help themselves, which might not be quite so convenient to the human "donor". We are all familiar with the mice which sometimes invade our houses in the winter seeking warmth and food, but we have had problems with a larger animal helping itself to food at our expense. For three winters we have had an otter ravaging our livestock. Our hens had been in a shed which was, to say the least, not at its best; it withstood the gales, but it could not keep out an otter and no matter how we tried to block the holes it was gradually dismantling the shed. It ripped off planks, dug underneath the sides and leapt up to climb in through a broken window. There was one bizarre incident, which has never been explained. One morning during this onslaught I went to repair the new hole at the back of the shed and what did I find rammed into it – a 3 lb pack of bacon. The bacon was fresh and not of a brand which we used, so how had it got there? We still do not know the answer. We could not picture any human feeling disposed to ram a 3 lb pack of bacon into the back of our shed; and yet why should an otter carry off the bacon and hide it there and then go in and grab a chicken?

It was not only the chickens who suffered at the teeth of the otter. We also lost our muscovy ducks, Kirsty's rabbits and a pair of geese. It is hard to imagine an otter tackling a fully grown gander, but it not only tackled it but succeeded in killing it and taking it away. And yes, we are sure it was the otter. It even had the blatant cheek to come and help itself to a hen in broad daylight and we saw it stalking the geese; on that occasion we were able to rush outside and scream at it to scare it away, but it returned when we were not watching and so we lost first the goose and then the gander. In the end we had to admit defeat and get a new "otter-proof" hen-house.

People often say the fox has to be killed because it takes chickens; the seal is shot because it takes the fishfarmers' fish and we are expected to understand and accept this. Yes, I fully understand the frustration of seeing where the animal has broken through again, but I cannot accept that this means the animal has to be killed. After all it is natural instinct (human as well as animal) to get a meal in the easiest way possible and so it is up to the livestock keeper or fishfarmer to protect his stock. The fact that the otter took our stock was not his fault – it was ours – we did not protect them enough and the otter took advantage of our slackness.

In the winter months we spend a lot of our time researching and repairing, but we spent the winter of 1985/86 building the museum which, at the time, was intended to display geological specimens, and later became an interpretation ??? providing a live video link to our otter pens. The building frame was pre-constructed but what a job it all was. It all started in November after months of planning, applying to building control, more planning, more changes and then finally the actual construction. The museum was made in kit form to high specifications to stand the incredible gales which can be thrown at the west coast. It had been designed by a local architect, who was originally from Iceland, and who was therefore used to these high standards, and I remember him saying "It will withstand anything once it is fully up". Little did I know how these words would echo in my head as time progressed. We laid the foundations, spending hour upon hour mixing concrete and pouring the stuff into the shuttered foundations. The building arrived and stood in sections on the driveway.

We arranged for some local builders to assemble it and on a sunny November morning they made a start and it began to go up very easily. Great, we thought, at this rate, it would soon be secure, but in the afternoon the news was interrupted by a staggering announcement: "Rockall Force 8 increasing force 9; Mallin Force 9 imminent; Hebrides Force 9 to Storm 10 imminent". We could not believe it – surely there was some mistake – it was so calm out there.

As yet, our two builders had not completed the construction; after all, to be fair it was planned to take about a week. That day when they left the structure looked incredibly high, propped up at the back like some huge sacrifice to the god of wind.

In the evening the wind increased and increased, and those words of the architect rang round in my head, keeping me awake all night. On many occasions as the gusts swept round the house, Paul ventured outside in his dressing gown to be lashed by wind and rain; his dimly lit torch peered at our building which was creaking and groaning in the strain of the gale. Not that there was much he could do if the whole lot came down in one almighty crash, but he just could not lie there listening to the howling winds.

In the morning the winds had died down and the sun peered through the receding clouds. We went outside and the sacrifice had been taken. Our building looked like some twisted contortion and there was little we could do.

Luckily the damage was not as severe as we had originally thought and the huge sections could be turned back and rebolted. We were also fortunate as that gale was a one-off and the rest of the building construction went smoothly without any major catastrophes.

The inside of the building created yet more headaches and looking inside the void it was hard to imagine that one day it would house an interpretation area. First we had to put down a floor. We borrowed a concrete mixer from a friend and then started again with the laborious task of concreting: mixing and filling and smoothing, mixing and filling and smoothing. (Anyone who has done a lot of concreting will understand exactly how tiring and boring it really is.)

The concreting did, however, have its compensations and on one fine March morning we both had an unforgettable experience. The sun was overhead taking the chill off the overnight frost. We dressed Kirsty, who was then nearly two, in warm old clothes and Paul started the archaic mixer; it was one of those diesel contraptions which took ages to come to life, and when it did, it throbbed and sent out loud shock waves of noise. Black smoke bellowed out of the exhaust as the old drum started to rotate and grind. We shovelled in sand, aggregate and cement, poured in water and the mixture turned and turned. "Ready for another barrow-load, Grace", Paul seemed to yell endlessly, turning off the clutch and pulling down the heavy wheel so that the sticky grey mixture dribbled into the barrow which was filled to capacity and wheeled away.

More sand, aggregate and cement went into the mixer and it churned and ground around. Paul came back, arms aching, clothes covered in the dust from the mixer. "What's that?" he said, looking out towards the bay. The head of what we thought was a small seal bobbed, and then disappeared. We continued with our work. As another load of concrete poured into the barrow, my eyes caught sight of a small cat sitting no more than 10 metres away from me on the gravel pathway. It was staring, totally transfixed by the diesel cement mixer, but it was not a cat – it was an otter. It did not look at all frightened, just inquisitive; then suddenly it seemed to notice us watching and ambled back towards the shore with the typical arched mustelid back. It plopped into the water and we watched for an hour as it swam up and down still attracted by the noise and commotion of the mixer. Finally it lost interest and swam on past Glas Eilean and away.

Little did we know at this time that these wonderful animals would play such an important part in our lives. We sat on the shoreline still hoping to catch another glimpse of it but to no avail. The mixer ground to a sudden halt and silence filled the beautiful landscape once more.

Chapter 4 ~ Grace

"THERE IS A LOVE OF WILD NATURE IN EVERYBODY, AN ANCIENT MOTHER LOVE EVER SHOWING ITSELF
WHETHER RECOGNISED OR NO, AND HOWEVER COVERED BY CARES AND DUTIES"
—JOHN MUIR

Each summer sees the main influx of human visitors to Skye and often we are asked where we would recommend going for a walk. This is not an easy question to answer. If the person is just after a fairly easy low-level walk, there are quite a few safe options, but when they say they are used to the hills it becomes more difficult. Do they mean hillwalking or climbing? And even the term "climbing" can mean different things to different people. On the one hand we do not want to insult someone's capability by sending them on a walk which they consider far too easy, but we also do not want to send them up some peak where they run the risk of getting into difficulties.

Every year lives are lost on the Cuillin hills: some accidents are caused by stupidity and inexperience when someone heads up the first hill they find without the necessary equipment or mountain knowledge; at other times conditions are such that even with the best knowledge and experience you are at risk. After all, the very word "accident" implies the unexpected and it is this which can kill even the best climber. All we can recommend is that no one considers going up the hills without adequate clothing, equipment and experience and without checking conditions as far as possible.

Sometimes the thoughtlessness of the "climber" does not actually cause an accident but creates inconvenience and potential risk. For example, three young men once told us they were going up Blaven and that if they were not back by five to ring the rescue services. Five o'clock came and no sign of them. We decided to give them an extra half hour as they may have been slightly delayed but when there was still no sign of them by half past five, we called the police, who said they would give them until six before assembling the Mountain Rescue Team, but just before six the three arrived at the door, safe and well and slightly merry. They had been down from the hill since four o'clock and had been sat in the pub since then. It never occurred to them that they should phone in and say they were back – they just enjoyed their pints. Obviously there was nothing wrong with relaxing and having a drink before returning, but one quick phone call would have saved so much needless worry and effort.

Walking, then, means a different thing to each and every individual and you can never take for granted what is expected in a "walk". One year, we were asked to take a group of 17 year olds on a day's walk. We were not exactly sure what was wanted, so gave them the choice of three different walks requiring differing degrees of fitness. They plumped for the walk to Camusunary which, for those who do not know it, is a Landrover track for three miles each way into an incredibly beautiful bay with a backcloth of the Cuillin peaks – probably one of the best walks into the hills without any danger but still providing great views. We pointed out to them that it was a Landrover track but that they would need walking boots, warm clothing and good waterproofs.

"Oh, that's fine," I was assured, "They will have been hillwalking in the Cairngorms before they reach you so they will be properly equipped."

"Fine," I thought, but I should have known better...

There were 27 of them with 4 adult supervisers. They arranged to pick me up at the Interpretation Centre at 10 a.m. Five past ten and the coach arrived and I clambered on. I sat next to one lad and immediately noticed that his "walking boots" consisted of a pair of tatty trainers. I was not impressed, but this turned to total disbelief when I got off the bus at Kilmarie and saw the full range of footwear. This lad's trainers were actually the best footwear of the lot and they ranged up to a young girl in a pair of high-heeled pink fluorescent boots. Their waterproofs were no better: a few had anoraks, but most had fashion jackets, which are supposed to be waterproof but certainly are not.

"Well, I'm afraid you can't go", I said to the girl in the pink boots – after all she would have broken her ankle within ten yards of starting the walk. I decided I would have to make the best of it, so we walked from the carpark to the gate and the start of the path.

Just inside the gate the path was very mucky: the cattle were being fed daily just here and so it was just one mess of mud and the unspeakable – ideal for trainers, I thought to myself. "We're not going", they all said in unison and slammed on the brakes. "Oh yes, you are," one of the supervisors told them. "No, we're not – we were told it was along a Landrover track", came the reply. I pointed out to them that Landrovers have this ability for driving off-road, but they simply turned round and headed back to the coach. "You're not getting back on the coach," they were told, but on they marched.

And so they argued. The pupils were adamant but so was their teacher and as I watched she sent the bus off to Broadford.

"We're still not going," came their defiant voices.

"Right then, you'll just stand here and get cold," was the reply.

During all this argument, one lad quietly said, "Well, I fancy going" and in the end, out of this group of 27 youngsters and 4 adults, I set off with him and 2 teachers. The rest just stood by the roadside for four hours and froze – it was March and although it was a nice day it was cold.

The four of us had a great walk. The views of the snowy peaks were superb and Tony, my sole student and a keen ornithologist, was rewarded with his first ever sight of a golden eagle.

Naturally, we got pretty mucky and when we got back Tony was met with a tirade of "Ugh – just look at the state of him". I could not resist it and retorted "Yes, but look at the state of you – at least his will wash off". I have always regarded young Tony as a strong character as it is not easy to stand up to your peers and decide to go against the flow. It is much easier just to give in and join them.

On other occasions people amaze you with their ability. We had another group who also requested a day walk and again they were given a choice of three possible walks. They chose the Storr – not just up to the Old Man but to the top of the Storr cliffs. When we met them we found they were nearly all well over 60 years of age and a couple of them looked as though they would barely be able to climb down out of the bus let alone go up the hill. But blow me, they all made it to the Old Man and then Paul took the fittest ones up on to the Storr and round whilst I took the others back down. Every single one of them was determined to make it at least to the Old Man and they wanted to see everything they possibly could on the way. The day did have one hiccup though, when on reaching the very top of the Storr cliffs, one of the party lost the use of his legs – a difficult situation on top of a cliff – resolved by Paul and one of the younger members accompanying the group having to carry him down. I have often mentioned the determination of these people to some of the "Moaning Minnies" you find in school groups, who are so used to being driven everywhere that they have virtually forgotten what their legs are for.

We live in a peculiar society where some people consider it a mental abnormality to walk when you have a car. And the same people will spend money and time "getting fit" at aerobics, using rowing and cycling machines, when all they need to do is to use their own power to achieve tasks like going to the shops and climbing the stairs.

We are fortunate that most of the guests on our own trips are concerned about our effect on wildlife and the environment in general. All too often, however, people simply do not care as long as they have exactly what they want when they want it. This can also apply to wildlife watching, as sometimes people are so concerned to see the particular species they seek that they really do not care if they disturb it. We have all seen pictures on television of safaris in Africa, but nowadays creatures like the cheetah cannot hunt in peace because every time they make a kill the word goes round on radios and a posse of vehicles arrives with an army of sightseers and the constant whirr of clicking cameras. Eventually the frustrated animal has to leave the meal to the hyenas and waste valuable energy trying to get another which it can enjoy alone.

We have seen the same sort of thing here. One year a corncrake decided to nest in the village and every night its rasping call could be heard by everyone passing down the road. This bird is becoming increasingly rare partly because of the loss of habitat and changing agricultural practices but also because of the change in climate and the widening of the Sahara desert, which it has to cross on migration. Whereas we once had corncrakes nesting throughout Britain nowadays they are more or less confined to the west coast of Scotland and the islands. Everyone was thrilled to hear our own corncrake until one evening when some selfish "twitcher", not content to hear it, had to see it and so went searching in the field. Next morning it was gone and who can blame it.

Television has greatly raised people's expectations. They are no longer content to see an eagle soaring as a dot in the sky. They have been treated to views of it sitting in the eyrie ripping meat to feed to its chicks, and they expect to sit down in the holt as the bitch otter feeds her cubs. There is, however, no substitute for the real thing and personally I would rather see the dot in the sky, knowing it is flying free and that I am seeing it for myself, than see the caged bird in a zoo or through the lens of someone else's camera.

In our work we always want people to have unforgettable wildlife experiences, but this must never be at the expense of the animal and its safety. Sometimes, however, we are able to show people sights they only thought they would see on TV, but we always try to leave the animal undisturbed.

On one occasion, we were sitting waiting for otters and, sure enough, one swam through the channel below us and disappeared. We sat a while longer and watched a small guillemot paddling away just yards offshore and then suddenly there was a flurry and it sank below the water. As we watched the otter surfaced and swam to the rocks just 6 metres from us where, it proceeded to eat the poor, unfortunate bird. We sat spellbound cringing at the sound of the crunching bones. After a good meal the otter stretched, rolled on the wet seaweed and settled down for a sleep on the rocks and we crept away feeling highly privileged to have seen this amazing spectacle.

Amongst the most curious of all species to watch is the human animal. We think we are so sophisticated and that we are the supreme beings but when we break it down we behave no better, and often a great deal worse, than the most "lowly" of our fellow creatures.

We watch spellbound as birds perform an elaborate courtship ritual, but do we ever look at ourselves? The female preens herself and sits watching as the male approaches. The male also preens himself, as well as makes himself bigger and shows off to other males, so that the female will be attracted to him. Now what are we talking about – a bird or a human? The pattern is the same.

We also have our territories firmly delineated. We may not go round and spraint like an otter so that other otters may know whose territory it is (that really would be beneath us). But instead we erect fences, not to keep livestock in or out, but merely to say "This is mine – keep out". In these days where we are trying to foster a feeling of one world, it shows how "animal" we really are if we have to erect a barrier to show it is our territory. And indeed no cock robin ever defended his territory more fiercely than we do.

This "territory" may not be just land. It can also be possessions. We all have possessions which we treasure and there is nothing wrong with that, providing it is not taken to extremes. But sometimes the extreme can be so extreme as to be bizarre.

We once had a lady staying with us who had come on holiday from the South of England and with her she had brought her treasured possession – a packet of frozen peas. Now this may seem a little bizarre to most of us, but to this lady these peas were of vital importance and they were to be guarded with great caution.

When she first arrived she asked if she could put these beloved peas into our freezer, which was of course no problem – we have had many strange requests. So off she went to fetch them from her room. In the meantime the rest of her family had somehow managed to lock themselves out of their room, which meant that Paul had to bring the ladders and climb into the room through the window. During all this commotion this dear lady was rushing about working herself into a frenzy crying "What about my peas? What about my peas?" No one really took any notice of her at this point, but eventually the room was unlocked and we took the peas, put them into the freezer and then set about calming our ruffled guest with a cup of coffee.

Every day during the course of her stay, our lady would come to the kitchen to check her peas and heaven help anyone if they had moved them from their rightful position in the freezer. They would be met with an icy stare and told in no uncertain terms "My peas should be over there".

When the time came for her departure, the peas were lovingly collected and placed into a cold bag for their careful journey home after their holiday. As far as we know the lady and the peas lived happily ever after.

Chapter 5 ~ Paul

"ABOUT HALF A LEAGUE TO THE NORTH OF PABBAY, LIES THE ISLE OF SHILLAY, A MILE
IN CIRCUMFERENCE, THAT YIELDS EXTRAORDINARY PASTURAGE FOR SHEEP. THEY HAVE THE BIGGEST
HORNS I HAVE EVER SEEN ON SHEEP."
—MARTIN MARTIN 1716

After some time of running trips on Skye, we decided to extend our programme to cover other areas of Scotland and to bring in the Outer Hebridean islands of Lewis and Harris. This meant we had to fit in trips to these islands in our so-called quiet season, namely October to March.

Lying west of Harris, way out in the Atlantic Ocean, are some small islands, and in late autumn large numbers of grey Atlantic seals haul out here to pup and then mate. The plan was to combine an autumn visit to Lewis and Harris with a trip to visit these grey seal colonies. But first it all had to be planned.

We had decided on possible accommodation on Lewis and we then tried to track down a boat which could take us out to the island of Shillay, lying 15 miles off Leverburgh at the southern tip of Harris. A hurried phone call made our final preparations.

"Hello, is that Mr Mackinnon? Is it still OK for you to take us over to Shillay next week?"

"Aye" replied Mr Mackinnon rather hesitantly.

"You said the journey would take about two hours each way?"

"Aye, it will depend a bit on the weather but it will be about four hours round trip, and then however long you want to land."

"Have you heard the forecast for next Monday?"

"Not yet, but I think we'll be all right."

"Well, let's hope so. Anyway there will only be three of us and we'll meet you at half past nine on the 24th."

"Aye, OK."

"Goodbye, Mr Mackinnon"

I left him on his tranquil island and we looked forward to leaving for Harris on the Caledonian MacBrayne ferry in a two day's time.

To reach the Outer Hebrides from Skye you have to drive to Uig and take the two-hour crossing to Tarbert on Harris. At times this means a crossing over the very stormy waters for which the Minch is infamous. And this was to be one such crossing!

We arrived at Uig in our faithful Landrover with plenty of time to catch the ferry. It was now 5.00 p.m. and the sun was illuminating the island with its very last rays. We loaded on our vehicle and in no time at all the ferry started moving and we steamed past Uig point.

Once we had left the safe haven of the harbour the wind began to pick up and we were soon rolling back and forth in the swell of the Minch. Fortunately, we are all good sailors and do not suffer from seasickness, but many passengers were soon turning green and disappearing, only to reappear in Tarbert, looking very pale and shaken.

On many of our subsequent trips to the Outer Hebrides it has been a joy to stand on deck and observe the abundant variety of wildlife from this very large ferry boat. If the sea is calm, we have seen killer whales, dolphins and a variety of seabirds. But on this occasion it was too rough to hope for much. However, in the dusky light we still saw numerous gannets diving on some of the very rich fishing grounds of these waters.

We arrived at Tarbert at 6.45 p.m. and drove the Landrover onto the island. It was pitch black and the lights of Tarbert shimmered in the rain which was now falling heavily – a total change from Uig. We searched for road signs but what we did not yet realise was that all the road signs are in Gaelic, while the maps are in English.

"There's a sign," Grace murmured.

The headlights swung onto the road sign to reveal the word Steornabhagh, which with a little imagination could be translated to read Stornoway. This was our road then, but things were not going to be that easy and we quickly learned that the Gaelic sounds do not readily translate to their English equivalent.

Gaelic was once widely spoken as far south as Northumberland. Over hundreds of years Gaelic has been suppressed to be replaced by English, and in many parts of Scotland it is now virtually extinct. Its stronghold is undoubtedly the Western Isles where it is used in day-to-day conversation, but recently there has been an upsurge in the language, which is very encouraging.

We drove on past Aird Asaig and began to realise that we had another problem. Some of the places marked on our map just did not appear to exist; we passed villages with beautiful sounding names like Aird a Mhulaidh and found ourselves at Baile Ailean. Grace shouted out that we had to turn right at Ballallan, so this must be the place. We drove up a windy lane into the darkness with not a house in sight until finally the dim lights of our hotel lit the road.

After a good dinner we settled down to an early night as tomorrow was going to be a long day.

We woke to sunshine which glistened as it spread its welcome rays on the loch below our window. In the bay a solitary harbour seal looked into the sky then disappeared, no doubt to look for fish. It popped up five minutes later and stayed almost motionless in the water before sinking again.

After breakfast we headed south to Leverburgh, hopefully, to meet Mr MacKinnon and his boat. The drive was very different from the night before, and daylight revealed some of the finest scenery of Lewis and Harris. We passed over the Harris hills with Clisham, the highest, standing like a sentry guarding the lochans below. On past Tarbert, we came to one of the most beautiful sandy beaches in the British Isles at Luskentyre on Harris – miles and miles of golden sand with not a beach umbrella to be seen. Finally we reached the southern tip of Harris at Leverburgh.

Originally the village had been called Obbe, but it had got its new name after Lord Leverburgh, who wanted to create a fishing and hand-loom industry here. Evidence of much construction can still be seen: it started in 1920 and was to consist of three quays, to harbour 200 fishing boats, as well as housing for the workers. However, Lord Leverburgh died in 1925 following a trip to the Congo and the work stopped in Leverburgh, as well as on various other schemes in Harris.

"There's a boat," shouted Kirsty and in the distance a lonesome fishing boat bobbed its way towards the pier.

Shillay is situated about 15 miles by sea from Leverburgh and has a healthy population of about 400 grey seals; together with its neighbouring islands, it forms the world "head-quarters" for this species. The island lies where the Sound of Harris widens out into the Atlantic ocean.

Grey seals are one of the largest of our British mammals and adult males can be up to 2 metres long. They have an elongated muzzle, paddle-shaped flippers at the front and fan-shaped ones at the rear. The very fat pregnant females gather in large groups in the early autumn and divide their time between basking on the shore and fishing. Just before giving birth they come ashore.

"Mr Mackinnon?" I called, as the boat tied up alongside the pier. "Aye," came the reply, "If you will get on board we will be leaving in about five minutes."

Soon we were away. The diesel engine chugged with a methodical thumping which seemed to blend in with the sounds of the sea and birds as the boat moved out of Leverburgh harbour and into the open waters. We passed the marker buoys set on rocks at the entrance to the harbour. Two common seals lay on the rocks and one moved its head ever so slightly to peer at us. It then set it down firmly on the ground again – obviously a boat was nothing new to him. Leverburgh was growing smaller and smaller and soon our boat started rocking and bobbing as some of the Atlantic swell hit her. Ahead of us lay the islands of Ensay and Killegray and in the distance Berneray and the northern tip of Uist.

An hour passed and Mr Mackinnon pointed to the rocks off the northern tip of Ensay which were full of cormorants and shags sitting like sentries – they must have numbered about 30 in total, and as the boat swept around they took off flapping their wings and beating the water for updraft, later to crash to the water and look up. These two species of bird look and act very similar and indeed occupy the same environment, so it is often difficult to distinguish the two. The cormorant is slightly larger but in summer they are easily identified as the cormorant has a white throat and thigh patch.

By now the boat was heaving and tossing heavily as it rode up and down on the swell, bobbing like a cork on the water. Mr Mackinnon stayed calmly at the helm and sat unconcerned with pipe in mouth, while the three of us just bounced about like loose beads in a bag. The island of Shillay was approaching and the engine throbbed on.

The rough water was beginning to get to Kirsty and she quietly said "Can we go home now?" However, with the promise of seeing seals she soon forgot about it and sat quietly waiting – not a common achievement for a two year old.

When we finally reached the island, what a sight for our eyes: the waters were alive with seals. The boat swung around away from the main colony and the anchor was set down near a sandy bay.

What always amazes me is the way a true Hebridean can rise to any occasion and Mr Mackinnon was not going to be outdone. He stood on deck tying little pieces of rope together to make a longer and longer strand. "There's a bit of a swell on," he said, as if there was just a gentle ripple.

I looked over to the shore and the waves crashed onto the sands of Shillay. Mr Mackinnon went on: "It will be difficult for you to row back against the swell, so if I tie the inflatable with this rope, I can pull you back should trouble arise."

If the rope holds, I thought to myself. He pulled out a rather small plastic inflatable and tied one end of the rope firmly onto the boat which he threw in the water. He continued to tie pieces of rope to the other end until in his mind the rope was about the right length.

It had been decided that, as Kirsty was then only two years old, only I should venture ashore, leaving Grace and Kirsty behind. So I climbed into the boat alone and started rowing. "Remember," shouted Mr Mackinnon, "I will pull you back with the rope. If the rope breaks I will throw you the man-overboard buoy – you should only get a little wet."

With that sort of encouragement I was full of confidence as I pulled away from the mother boat. As I rowed on, the seals appeared all around me and I ended up rowing right amongst them with their heads appearing every so often near to the oar. I think I lost count at about 45 in the water. At times it was quite frightening, as when a bull grey seal appeared out of the water about one metre away. After all, these are large animals, about 2 metres long weighing about 230 kilogrammes. I was nearing the land and the inquisitiveness of the seals had waned. With one final rush of a rather large wave, the inflatable hurtled towards the shore and crashed onto the sand.

Shillay is not a large island and is only 80 metres high at its north west corner. It is an island which has never been tamed by man and only the yearly arrival of the seals brings it to life.

If I think of all the marvels of nature, nothing will stay in my memory more than this trip – the island was littered with young seals, their coats as white as snow but nevertheless their teeth as sharp as nails. Mothers lay nearby guarding these precious babies, which they tended and nursed so caringly. I was careful not to disturb them as it is very easy to break the bond between a mother and pup and once this has been broken the mother will abandon it and the pup will eventually die of starvation. Quite often the public can interfere with seals and take a young seal pup off the shore. It is however quite normal for a mother to leave her pup for a while and the message is always 'leave well alone' – if you must do anything, then just observe.

I moved very slowly around the outside of the colony which was spread far inland. Many pups were on the sand whilst others were a hundred yards up on the grassy hillside. A small bank gave me a good vantage point and I looked over to observe a large female who was just a few metres away. She groaned and rolled on the grass and in 15 minutes a small red and white object appeared which was no more than one metre long and weighed, I am sure, no more than 14 kilogrammes. The female keeled over to one side as the pup made feeble attempts to find the nipples which would supply it with vital food for the next three weeks. In order to aid streamlining a seal has inverted nipples and as long as the pup can fumble in the correct vicinity the nipples will pop out. This pup latched on within 15 minutes, but many can take much longer. It suckled for 10 minutes, changing nipples before snuggling into his mother and falling very gently asleep.

This pup will double in weight in the first week putting on some 1.5 kilogrammes per day. At the end of lactation, some 18 days later, it will be three times its birthweight, but the mother suffers drastically and will lose much of her fat by the time she leaves her offspring.

While all this is going on the males are lurking in wait, and now on Shillay many had already started to congregate on the distant shore. The large bulls were strategically positioned as if on some giant game board, for which I had no idea of the rules. All was quiet until one tried to move on to another's square and then the sparring began for a position in the breeding hierarchy.

Once the little pup is weaned the female will be put into a harem of about ten controlled by one dominant male. Quite often fights between the males can break out and in some cases this can be very aggressive with gruesome bites and bloody wounds. On this occasion all was calm and just one male barked aggressively at another which moved quickly away.

After mating the female will leave the land and go back into the sea, her true environment, leaving her pup onshore. The pup will soon venture slowly into the water and learn to hunt and fend for itself – but this will all take time and patience.

Meanwhile the fertilised egg in the mother will start dividing, but development is suspended for four months until she moults. The egg will then be implanted and normal development will continue. Everything in nature is always done for a purpose and since grey seals spend the great majority of their lives at sea, when they do come onto land they have to have everything synchronised; the four month delay allows for pupping, weaning and mating to occur at the correct time of year.

The island of Shillay that day was such a sight. The sky above was blue and all around were seals: some wailed, others slept and in the distance a large male grunted. I had spent just two hours on the island and time was short. The day was drawing in and I reluctantly headed back to the inflatable. The Atlantic swell had increased and the waves lashed onto the shore in cascades of white foam.

I pushed the boat out as wave after wave made me wetter and wetter. Mr Mackinnon pulled at the thin rope as I rowed clumsily and we started to make ground. After the splash zone it was much easier going and it was not long before I was dripping on the deck of the boat.

"The last time I took people out here was for the seal cull," said Mr Mackinnon. "That would have been a good five years ago or maybe more. It was in the days when fur coats from seals were fashionable and rather trendy down in the cities, but we like the creatures and to enjoy them is a better way than to kill them."

In fact, the seals on most of these islands used to be killed on a regular basis, and the seal products were used for various meaningless items. The flesh was not really eaten by humans, and, indeed, Martin Martin wrote in the account of his epic trip to the Outer Hebrides in the 1600s, "the seal is esteemed only for the vulgar". Seal flesh was occasionally used as lobster bait. The fur was made into tourist trinkets and surely nothing can be more indicative of our uncaring society than to sell toy seals wrapped in real seal fur to children. But thank goodness those days have long since gone in our country – haven't they?

The engine of the boat throbbed into action and our wooden boat very slowly twisted round. I glanced back and watched through binoculars at my pup feeding from its mother. I say "my" because to experience that wonder of nature first hand gives you a bond with that animal which lasts with you for a life time.

The island was fading as the boat headed on to Leverburgh and we said goodbye to the seals, the masters of Shillay and the sea.

Chapter 6 ~ Paul

'ONLY BY GOING ALONE IN SILENCE WITHOUT BAGGAGE CAN ONE TRULY GET INTO THE HEART OF THE WILDERNESS. ALL OTHER TRAVEL IS MERE DUST AND HOTELS AND BAGGAGE AND CHATTER'

—JOHN MUIR

With our great love of islands, our next step was to explore and organise holidays to the Small Isles; these are the islands which nestle in an arc between Skye and the Outer Hebrides. On many a fine day, you feel you can almost touch the islands of Eigg, Muck, Rhum and Canna as you look across the Inner Sound from Skye, but getting to them without your own boat can take you a day in itself.

You reach the Small Isles with the Caledonian MacBrayne ferry from the busy fishing village of Mallaig. In the summer season there is also a car ferry from the mainland to Mallaig and the pier is always crowded with empty fish boxes, rucksacks and booted climbers all waiting for the boats to appear.

Eigg is the first island visited by the Small Isles ferry and has a quite unique profile with An Sgurr rising nearly 400 metres. After much careful planning, our first party was about to board the *Lochmor* bound for this lovely little island. The day was not one of the better ones which the Hebrides can offer and a cold but at least dry wind blew from the north. The fishing boats bobbed up and down in the harbour and as one boat left the shelter it started to tilt and sway, as it sailed out followed by a group of friendly herring gulls in its wake. Our journey to Eigg was to take about one and a half hours and we loaded our kit on board and waited impatiently for the ferry to leave.

Ropes were cast off and carefully coiled, and plumes of smoke bellowed from the diesel engines as we manoeuvred around the fishing boats and then ventured full ahead and out into the Sound. We looked over to Ardvasar on Skye with its white cottages gripping the hillside. In front of us on the mainland were the beautiful white sands of Morar, but on that day they looked bleak and dreary as clouds moved in from the west.

Suddenly the full force of the swell hit us and the *Lochmor* lurched to the side and back again as time and time again the bow was hit by large rollers. It heaved up and over wave after wave and soon one or two of our guests began to look a bit worse for wear. As someone who fortunately does not suffer from the dreaded seasickness my heart goes out to those who do, but really you can do no more than comfort them and give them clean bags.

I can remember on another occasion when the wind backed to a force 8 and the *Lochmor* tossed and turned as the rollers pounded her side. A French lady was on board for the round trip, which would take seven and a half hours. We were only ten minutes out of Mallaig and as I struggled down to the galley to get a cup of coffee there she was, flat on the floor uttering in a dramatic French accent, "I want to die, I want to die." At Eigg she insisted on going ashore even though the captain repeatedly told her that the next boat was not due for two days, weather permitting. But she would have none of it. Without accommodation or a change of clothing we watched her disappear into the small harbour of Eigg.

The first impression of Eigg, as the boat begins to hug the coastline, is of a rather austere island with sheer cliffs rising almost straight from the sea, but as the ferry heads for a gap in the cliffs a cluster of trees give a hint at the gentler side to the island. On the right of the little harbour is the whitewashed Kildonan farm, which we also use as a base for some of our trips. It was here that 1300 years ago St Donan brought Christianity from Ireland and founded a monastery.

The *Lochmor* cannot enter the shallow harbour, and so people, cases and all supplies have to be unloaded onto a small launch, which was now chugging out to meet us. On many occasions this is a pleasant and simple transfer but with the present swell it might have caused a few problems. The launch tried to come into the side of the *Lochmor* but had to pull away; it tried again at another angle but no, the swell was too much. The *Lochmor* turned around a little to try to shield the small boat and a final approach was made. This time it was successful but the wee boat bobbed up and down rising up almost 2 metres and then dropping down 2 metres. My party looked at me in sheer amazement; Mary, a wonderful lady of 75 years, who was a regular visitor and joined us every year, looked shocked.

The transfer was as dramatic as it looked: the crew held both arms, shouted "go" as the boats came level and threw us into the arms of the men on board the launch. To our surprise we soon found that we were all safe aboard the small launch. Then bags and baggage, a sack of mail, a coil of fencing wire and various boxes of groceries and vegetables joined us in the bottom of the boat until finally we were chugging away from the mother ship.

Whenever you go to Eigg there is always a small crowd gathered on the pier to meet the boat. After all, this boat is not only bringing visitors. All post, food and supplies have to travel this way. So as we approached the harbour cars appeared, some with doors and wings missing, lost in the ravages of the wind. Then we gratefully stepped foot on the Isle of Eigg.

Eigg is a strangely-shaped island, measuring five miles long but no more than three miles wide. In the 18th century it was owned by a gun-runner, Lawrence Thompson, who sold arms to the Japanese amongst others, and he has left a legacy in the grand appearance of the Lodge House and the fort-like building by the pier. In fact, the man himself also owned the neighbouring island of Muck and the Strathaird peninsula on Skye and is reputed to have been buried standing upright to look over his kingdoms bought with this corrupt money.

Today Eigg lies peaceful, the gem of the Small Isles. We set off to Laig farm, which was to be our base for the next week, in a Landrover which showed all the signs of having had a hard life. It chugged up the hill to the post office billowing out plumes of black smoke both outside and inside the vehicle.

After stopping for a while to collect the post, we went on over Bealach Clithe and in front lay Laig Bay with Cleadale to the right and Laig farm nestling below the crags of Blar Dubh. And beyond, the Isle of Rhum stood like a sentinel keeping watch on its gentle neighbour, while its own landscape lay bare and rugged from the contortions and geological upheaval over the eons of time.

After settling in, we ventured out for a short walk before supper along the sands of Laig Bay. We continued around the coast to Camas Sgiotaig with its clear crisp "singing sands", so-called because when dry they "squeak" as you walk. Curlew and oystercatchers played among the kelp as one or two of the party skated along the sands hoping its white quartz grains would play some Hebridean symphony for them.

Looking up from the bay you can see the great landslip of Cleadale, giving shelter to the small crofting township during the worst of the winter storms. The landslip was formed some 40 million years ago by the huge weight of basalt lavas on the soft Jurassic sediment, which just could not take the strain. They eventually gave way to produce this wonderful chaotic scenery and rich soils, which support a great array of alpine flowers. It is not just the flora which is enhanced by this geological extravaganza as the crags form ideal habitat for ravens with buzzards and golden eagles soaring overhead. And there are also the Manx shearwaters which nest beneath the cliff face in old rabbit burrows. These comical birds take it in turns to sit on the eggs and change the sittings at night, so as not to be caught by the waiting raptors. On a suitable night you can sit below the cliffs and listen to these birds flying in from the sea calling out to locate their burrows with eerie screams like laughing witches.

As we ambled along the shore, one of our party spotted a lonesome great northern diver in the bay and we put up the telescope to see this bird in more detail. It was rolling in the water to preen, and as it did so, we saw clearly its clean white underparts. These birds are mainly winter visitors to our waters and would soon be leaving to spend the summer and breed in Greenland and Iceland.

It was time to head back. It had started to drizzle and within an hour rain lashed into the farmhouse windows with a tremendous ferocity. That night we went to bed with the rain still pouring, and as the farmhouse generator stopped, nothing could be heard but the force of the rain on my attic window.

In the morning I woke to the sound of a buzzard mewing over the farm, and clinks of sunlight pierced through the cloudy sky. The rain had stopped and the small burn below the cottage rushed with new water.

On our first full day on the island we were setting off to Galmisdale and on to the Massacre Cave at the southern end of Eigg. We left the farm, rejoined the road towards the pier, and then took the path over to the cave. The entrance to this cave of St Francis

is small and a wooden cross stood as a tribute to the terrible events which happened here in 1577.

The story has many versions but the traditional account tells how a boat owned by the Macleods was forced to land in bad weather. Eigg belonged to the Macdonalds, the arch enemies of the Macleods, and when the boat crew asked for food and shelter they were refused and set adrift.

Weeks past and the Macleods of Skye returned seeking revenge. They arrived and looted and burned the houses as their inhabitants fled and hid in the cave. The Macleods left and a scout was sent out from the cave to watch their departure, but unfortunately he was spotted by one of the Macleod crew. The boats turned back to shore and the Macleods followed the tracks of the scout back to the hiding place. There they lit a fire in the mouth of the cave and suffocated the island population of 398.

We ventured through the narrow entrance and on as it widened out into a large cavern which could easily hold 400 people. What a terrible way to die, trapped in this hole under the earth. In 1845 Hugh Miller, the lay preacher and geologist, visited Eigg and described in detail the piles of bones, lying as if in family groups. Soon after, they were collected and buried; however, a child's skull was still found in the cave as late as 1970.

We were all filled with a chilly sense of sadness and were glad to retrace our steps. The dim light from the entrance could be seen and we clambered out to be greeted by gleaming sun and the sound of the sea lapping happily on the rocks below. We sat quietly having our lunch on the shore that day – somehow you cannot help but be moved by this cave and its memories.

As we went home over the Bealach that afternoon, the cloud was slowly creeping in over Rhum and wisps of grey drifted towards us. With these clouds came a light breeze which whipped up the calm sea before us and blew a cooling chill over our bodies. It would not be long before the rain appeared, and we hurried back for our evening meal.

I could go on talking about this wonderful island. We are indeed fortunate to visit at least on a yearly basis and experience its ever changing moods and character.

On our return ferry to Mallaig, the *Lochmor* worked its way around Muck and Rhum and then Canna. Canna – this was an island which looked so enchanting and inviting and as we steamed away we promised ourselves to visit Canna the following year.

For wildlife, Canna is spectacular, with the second highest cliffs in Britain, which teem in seabirds: they are littered with guillemots, razorbills kittiwakes and puffins. Shag colonies surround the rugged coastline and the white-tailed sea eagle sometimes soars overhead. We have had many memorable trips to this magical island but I will try to capture a day which will always stay in my mind – the very first day I stepped foot on Canna.

I was going ahead as an advanced party of myself and Kirsty, who was then four years old, to spend a weekend on the island to prepare for the group when they arrived on the Monday afternoon. We had to spend Friday night in Mallaig as we had no way of getting to Mallaig from Skye in the early hours of Saturday morning. We booked into the Caledonian Hotel, which is near the ferry terminal, so that we would not have a long walk to reach the Canna ferry, which left at the unsociable hour of 5 a.m. on the Saturday morning.

We woke bright and early and settled down to the breakfast tray they had left for us. Kirsty wasn't hungry – excitement had taken hold of the little girl and she hastily packed her bag. "What time does the ferry go, Dad?" she must have asked me about a hundred times. If the truth be known I was also excited and not really hungry although as adults we have a better way of hiding it – or at least pretending to. The sun had not yet fully risen as we crept out of the hotel front door and a chilly wind blew the salty air into our faces. Mallaig harbour was cluttered with fishing boats of all shapes and sizes, moving ever so gently on the water. It was so different to see them in these conditions so early in the morning; usually the harbour is filled with the hustle and bustle of fishing activity.

Caledonian MacBrayne had not as yet put on its summer service and the faithful *Lochmor* was having her yearly overhaul, so the *Pioneer*, a much larger vessel, was going to take us to Canna. We boarded the boat and promptly at 5 a.m. she started her two and a half hour trip straight out to Canna and then on to the other members of the Small Isles group.

Herring gulls hovered overhead and the local grey seal, which scavenges on the leftover fish of the harbour, popped its head out of the water. We passed the small light marking the rocks and moved out of the harbour entrance, which was patrolled by shags draping their wings to dry in the rising sun.

After an hour of sailing, the island of Canna could be seen vaguely, but we could only make out a hazy idea of its shape. It rose out of the water then disappeared as the *Pioneer* steamed on, like some large humpback whale. By now the sun had risen and what a sight it was – the Island of Rhum to our left, Eigg behind on the horizon and the Cuillins of Skye, still peppered with snow, etching into the skyline. I could feel it in my bones that this was going to be a special weekend. To land on Canna is like a homecoming, with its sheltered peaceful harbour, the green fertile fields and the crags leading to the magnificent sea cliffs.

Canna has been treated as a bird sanctuary since 1938; 157 species have been recorded over the years and the experts say that something like 71 species have bred, including the sea eagle and other species of birds of prey.

As the boat tied up at the pier, we could make out our home for the next week, which lay in the woods above Canna House. Canna was given to the National Trust for Scotland by Dr Lorne Campbell who owned the island but he and his wife still lived in the impressive Canna House. Our home was to be Tigh Ard, the house on the hill built in 1905.

We were met by a Landrover which took us up the hill to the house and we settled in. The house has a grand appearance and was to be the base for our group when they arrived on Monday. It has five large bedrooms and servant quarters and was set in a magnificent wooded garden.

I was busy unpacking when a voice called out in the distance, "What are these, Dad?" Then bells started ringing as my explorer daughter proceeded to ring all the attendant's bells in the bedrooms, which went directly to alert the servants in the kitchen.

Kirsty and I stood by the large picture window of the master bedroom, overlooking tranquil Canna harbour. The ferry had long gone and all was quiet. Two otters played amongst the kelp looking for the small fish which supply most of their diet. It was now 8.30 a.m. and with not a cloud in the sky we could tell the day was going to be a scorcher.

We had much to do, so we packed our rucksack and made our way over to the island of Sanday which is about a four mile walk. Sanday is connected to Canna by a small footbridge which can be damaged in extreme gales, leaving the island isolated from mainland Canna at high tide. At low tide it is possible to go across the sands in wellies.

We walked over the little wooden footbridge and onto the island, passed some of the disused cottages and stopped to look at the little schoolhouse. What a wonderful building – no road to it, grass right up to the front gate, with a "School" sign on the shore. The school was built in 1878, and at that time it had 20 pupils. On this day there were only 2 and eventually this number was to dwindle even further as politics and bad management led to the closure of the school. Before that was to happen, however, our daughter was to have much pleasure being taught there during our brief stays with groups. Hamish and Iona have long since gone but they were some of her best friends. I can remember watching them all play over on a distant hill on Canna – but that is probably only nostalgia.

We left the school and headed past the empty croft houses and over towards Dun Easubric, making our way over the hill. The sight was absolutely breathtaking with fulmars, kittiwakes, razorbills and guillemots lining the rock faces.

We sat watching the fulmars dart in and out of the cliff face, with their straight wings moving on the air currents. Today the islands of Sanday and Canna possess some 500–600 fulmar but they have only colonised the islands, like most of Britain, in the last hundred years and the original colony was on the remote St Kilda archipelago. On the far crags the kittiwakes fussed about on their ledges. These are remarkable gulls in that they look so clean and gentle with their grey and white plumage and dark eyes. Once you have been near a colony, the "kittiwa-ak" call will be fixed in your mind for ever as it is uttered time and time again as the birds bicker over their nest sites. Take time to watch them carefully and you will see intruders constantly flying up to sitting birds; they both greet each other and the intruder flies off. Their nests, which are so delicately and carefully made, are built of seaweed on very small ledges.

We lay down near Dun Beag watching puffins come and go from the sea. Of all the auks, these beauties are the most comical, with their coloured bills which do in fact go darker in the non-breeding season. The kittiwakes went on calling "kittiwa-ak, kittiwa-ak". The last I remember was being mesmerised by this call and I woke up about two hours later. Kirsty was still asleep to this symphony of seabirds.

It was now about 3 p.m., the sun was still hot and there was a lot of daylight left. "Please Dad, can I go for a swim?" Kirsty asked once she had come to. "Oh please, Dad, please." I was eager to explore some other areas but the tranquillity of the islands, the sun and the warmth made me give in to her (or, to be honest, to myself) and we walked along to a sandy beach where she spent the whole afternoon in the sea.

It was wonderful to watch Kirsty play, backdropped by the Cuillins of Rhum. No artificial roundabouts or swings, expensive toys, mechanical gismos which people think are necessary to please children; all she needed was just sand and sea and the odd puffin or two bobbing in the water to keep her company.

Eventually we headed home over the little footbridge and on to Canna, through the farm and over the fields past the Cross. This marks the site of the original chapel to St Columba which was situated within the pre-clearance village of Keil. We carried on up the hill and home to Tigh Ard.

Over the years we have been to Canna many times and the weather has nearly always been glorious, but I don't think any visit there will last in my memory like this first day with my daughter. Because it takes so long to get there, Kirsty thinks it is abroad and on a regular basis packs her shorts, swimming costume and no warm sweaters. Today, with her friends gone, it has no school and no children to spend time with on the long warm summer evenings, but still when we say "Kirsty, we are off to Canna on Saturday", we are always met with the same excited, "Yes!"

Chapter 7 ~ Paul

"TO ME IT WAS PEACE LIVING ON ST KILDA AND TO ME IT WAS HAPPINESS, DEAR HAPPINESS."

—MALCOLM MACDONALD, ONE OF THE EVACUEES

It was some ten months later that we set foot on Canna again, heading out this time to the far off St Kilda in a converted fishing trawler. The islands of St Kilda lie some 45 miles north west of Uist and like many remote places they hold an incredible fascination for people. St Kilda is the most distant group of islands in Britain with their stark grandeur and bleak, towering cliffs (the highest in Britain) standing out of the stormy Atlantic. They have a special mystique which only a visit will cure, and this is why a group of us set sail from Oban on that sunny Saturday in June on board the *MV Kylebhan*. The account below was written during that trip and we hope you will share with us some of our delights and reservations.

Way back on 29 August 1930, St Kilda was overcast and grey, with a cold, sharp mist coming in from the sea. It was not only the day the St Kilda Post Office closed, but the very day the islands on the edge of the world were evacuated, and the last remaining 36 citizens removed to areas new. This community, which had survived alone and isolated in the Atlantic for centuries, was finally brought down by the ravages of the modern world. On 30 August, the national papers had bold headlines "Exodus from St Kilda", and for those who looked on at the evacuation of this isolated community, it was a victory for their own social order. (The St Kildan were like an ancient tribe of people. To the upper classes of England it was an embarassment to have people living in such primitive conditions, even though they may have been happy and contented.) For the St Kildans, it was the end of their unique way of life – a life of survival amidst the hardships of nature.

Our crossing would take two days and we set out from Oban in warm sunshine, passing Mull, where we stopped briefly to top up the water supply. We arrived in Canna harbour in the early evening, which was still lit up by the last rays of sunshine.

We awoke the next morning to find the weather had taken a turn for the worst, and we left Canna in the early hours of a wet and windy Sunday morning, feeling more than just a little apprehensive as to what the Minch and Atlantic would throw at us. We were not disappointed. We pitched and tossed in a heavy swell, which made us all hold on for safety, and the cold northerly wind chilled those who ventured onto deck. We passed through the Sound of Harris and there was the Isle of Shillay to our right. The Atlantic seals had long since gone and the sandy beach and moorland seemed bare without the sights and sounds of those wonderful creatures. But it would only be five months before the yearly cycle will begin again and the seals will return from all corners of the seas to have their young.

At 10 p.m. There was a shout from the deck as St Kilda peered out, draped in mist with a rich glow of deep orange sun cascading behind the high hills: Boreray and Stac Lee to our right, and then Hirta, the main island, with Soay peeping from behind, and Dun to our left. We all stood on deck staring as the last drops of light faded from the sky, but it was another hour and a half until we anchored in Village Bay, tired, cold and in need of sleep.

The archipelago of St Kilda is believed to take its name from a mistake in a translation of the old Norse *Skildir* (Shields) which appears on older maps to have been associated with one of the offshore islands near the Hebrides.

The earliest human habitation on the islands is believed to have been in about 2000 BC, in the Bronze Age. These people probably came from Harris and Uist, bringing with them their domestic animals, such as sheep and goats, and supplementing their diet with fish, seals, seabirds and their eggs. Martin Martin produced the first written account when he visited the islands in 1697 and at this time the population had risen to about 180. The main village was moved nearer to the sea and the curving line of 'new' cottages were being repaired by the National Trust work parties when we landed on Hirta on Monday morning.

Our own first impressions were strange: the islands are alive with seabirds – puffins, fulmars, razorbills, gannets and the great skua patrolling the airways looking for scraps of food to steal or unguarded eggs or chicks. In the distance the bare landscape was extensively overgrazed by the native Soay sheep and dotted all over with cleats – these strange-looking structures so important to the old St Kildan life as store rooms for the many seabirds harvested by the islanders. But above the pier lay the huge monstrosity of the army camp, with its dire grey buildings despoiling the site of the old village. The skyline above was dominated by aerial masts and domes scanning the skies for missiles fired from Uist – structures totally out of place in Britain's only World Heritage Site.

Just over 60 years ago, the St Kildan people lived a happy but harsh life on these islands, harvesting the seabirds which now make the island so important for tourists. Although cultivation was poor, barley and oats were grown in small areas, and the islands managed to sustain a population which peaked at 200 people with some 1000–2000 Soay sheep. It was in the nineteenth century that the tourist ships began to arrive and the people traded tweeds, knitwear and sealskins for their independence. The growth of a money-based economy was their downfall and they became more and more dependent on provisions from afar.

Today the islands have a tripartite ownership: in 1956 the Marquis of Bute left the islands in his will to the National Trust for Scotland, so that they might keep them for the benefit of the nation. The Trust agreed to lease them to the government's Nature Conservancy Council, who in turn let the military lease a little and destroy a lot.

We walked through the village, busy with people from the Trust's work party pointing walls which were originally drystone, passed the museum with its collection of memorabilia and on towards the Isle of Dun. Puffins, fulmar and guillemots filled the skies like flies, always busy, always moving. The clear blue sea below us glistened with seabirds, carpeting the ocean like flowers. We continued along the cliffs which drop sharply into the thundering Atlantic and it was here two days later that a pod of Orca whales rose and plunged into the sea. We counted five, including two males with their huge, pointed dorsal fins, and one young protected by its ever-loving mother. They swam eastwards and continued on past the edge of Soay and out of sight. We could not help but marvel at the wonderful diversity which nature has to offer, great skuas filled the sky above us with strange calls of anger as we ventured past their nests. They dived at us from great heights sometimes just missing the top of our heads; and out to sea, the mighty giant Orca, whose quiet magnificence leaves you speechless.

Our next day was a trip out towards the giant northerly stacks of Stac an Armin and Stac Lee, which hold one of the most important gannet breeding stations in the world. The anchor was slowly pulled up by our crew and the *Kylebhan* was once again set free from Village Bay, ready to ride on the Atlantic waters. First we circumnavigated the islands of Hirta, Dun and Soay, with their magnificent cliffs crowded with birds, and then headed out to the stacks, our boat rolling slightly in the now gentle swell. We soon found ourselves in the lee of the stacks and above our heads more gannets than you could ever imagine. To the left rose Stac Lee, a sheer rock, white with gannets, where the noise and smell were almost overpowering.

Our boat continued beneath skies full of birds plummeting down and then rising up from the water's depths. We stopped for a while beneath the cliffs where the waters were calmed by the shelter of a small cove and we watched bewitched – not only gannets but puffins, razorbills, kittiwakes and guillemots. So many people miss out on the full experience by just ticking birds – the real pleasure comes in watching quietly as they perform their daily duties. The importance of watching was brought home as we looked at the guillemots and we noticed how like penguins they really are, not just in looks but also in their antics: several times we watched as they rose with the surge of water to leap clear onto the rocks as the waves dropped back; they then proceeded to jump up the rocks in true rockhopper penguin style until they reached a ledge. To merely tick them as a guillemot would have meant the loss of so much. But then St Kilda is not a place for "ticking". Yes, there are unusual species, like Leach's petrel, but the fascination for birdwatchers lies largely in the countless numbers.

In spite of its daily battles over food and territory and its noisy chatter, peace for human beings truly reigns in this world of birds. If ever there was anywhere to experience true peace on earth, then surely it is here. The Atlantic, that foaming mass of water, has been laid calm by ancient forces which threw up these wonderful rock outcrops from the very bowels of our earth. On every rock stands a bird, the very sun itself can hardly penetrate to your face which is shadowed by the incredible number of gannets.

As we left this tranquil place and headed back to Village Bay, with its hustle of military activity, a helicopter circled overhead bringing in some high flying personnel to spend the night drinking in the military pub.

In 1987 the islands were awarded the grand recognition of "World Heritage Site", and within two months planning permission was sought for bigger and grander domes and aerials on the hill of Mullach Mor. The Western Isles Council rightly turned them down, even though the islands' owners, the National Trust for Scotland, did not even object. However, the Western Isles Council's decision was overruled by the Scottish Secretary of that time, Malcolm Rifkind, and the building went ahead – vast monuments to war and destruction on this beautiful archipelago.

On leaving St Kilda a sense of sorrow was felt by all. Yes, this spectacular set of islands is unique with its scenery and birdlife; it holds within its sheer cliff boundaries the remains of a community whose way of life survived until 1930. Until then human being and animal alone defeated the bleak, savage environment, but then the tourist ships appeared which looked on the population as peculiar museum specimens to be stared at and patronised. The defeat and ultimate evacuation of the people of St Kilda was the start of the island's decay and has destroyed the very reason why St Kilda should be a World Heritage Site.

If we have lost anything, we have lost our sense of purpose in a world where often hate runs deeper than love. Our mighty military machine has fuelled an alarming arms race in post war Britain, trading weapons of destruction to countries who cannot even afford to feed their own people; and even in St Kilda the high technology of war has replaced a severe but peaceful way of life and has etched its way into the natural beauty of the islands at the edge of the world.

Some argue that without the military presence, the work of the conservation bodies would be difficult. Yes, they do a lot of good for the people working there, but surely if we have funds for these weapons of destruction, the same funds could be found for peaceful activities.

We recognise the importance of the islands by designating them as a World Heritage Site, National Nature Reserve, Special Site of Scientific Interest, and the village is protected by the Ancient Monuments Society; and yet we allow all this to be spoiled by the modern monuments of war.

As we neared the Sound of Harris on our return journey, St Kilda was a distant view, small, fading and hazy, and I recalled Findlay McQueen's words as he left his island home: "May God forgive those who have taken us away from St Kilda". As the archipelago disappeared, I wondered if God ever did.

Clockwise from top left:

Fran the fox
Sammy the seal
Otter swimming in the sea off Kyleakin (*Photo: Tom Balks*)
Eurasian Otter, Sleat Peninsula, Skye (*Photo: Emil Barbelette*)
Weighing a hedgehog

Clockwise from top left:
Lewis, a young otter cub
Tiny hedgehog
Otter in kelp
Short-eared owl in the aviary
Kirsty, Ben and Connaire camping in the garden

Clockwise from top left:

Su, a young otter cub
Ben, Connaire and Kirsty (*Photo: Mark Yoxon*)
Tawny owlet
Eurasian Otter, Sleat Peninsula, Skye (*Photo: Emil Barbelette*)
Tawny Owl

Wildlife Study Group, near our home in Broadford

Chapter 8 ~ Grace

It was that trip to St Kilda which got us really close to whales and in particular the Orca. We had encountered them on many occasions before but not so close, giving such wonderful views. Two pods of Orca whales passed close to our boat off Heisker – these must be amongst the most magnificent of whales seen in our waters. It was also the St Kilda voyage which gave us memorable sightings of bottle-nosed dolphins riding on the bow wave of the boat. We first picked them up about half a mile away and they were making a bee-line straight towards our boat; before long they were riding on the bow wave at the front of the boat, so close you could almost touch them. They stayed there for about five minutes rising and disappearing as our boat ploughed on. The human party was in a state of utter excitement as everyone hung over the sides in various precarious positions, snapping cameras at these agile mammals. Then one by one the dolphins peeled off and disappeared into the distance behind us.

Our first ever encounter with a whale, however, was from the window of our own house during our very first year on Skye and took place in the month of June. It was 7 a.m. on a Sunday and all was quiet and peaceful. I opened the curtains to a bright and sunny day with the water lying calm as a mirror.

"It will be a good day for Paul and the group today," I thought. "Camusunary will be cracking on a day like this." For those of you who have never been there, Camusunary is a wonderful sandy bay, in the heart of the Cuillin mountain range.

I pulled on my clothes and went downstairs to lay the tables for breakfast. As I glanced out of the dining room window with a handful of knives, I saw something which

made me look again. There was something dark in the water. Now I am not at my best in the mornings – in fact, normally I am barely conscious – and to me in that state it looked as if someone was out in a small boat. Then suddenly it sank! Oh no, I thought, it is so calm today surely nothing can have happened to the boat. But then as I watched transfixed to the spot, it rose again a few metres away. Now even when I have just woken up I know that boats do not sink and rise again! And slowly it began to dawn on me that this dark object was alive and rising and falling in the water naturally. I watched for a few more seconds and, sure enough, I saw a dark fin on the back. At this point I ran through to Paul in a state of great excitement.

We went outside clutching our binoculars and in the still morning air we could hear the whoosh of water as the animal blew on reaching the surface.

The identification of whales and dolphins can be very difficult: the Orca is quite distinctive with its large dorsal fin, but some of the other whales are really hard to identify, particularly as often you only get fleeting glimpses of the dorsal fin as it glides out of the water. This animal we estimated to be about 5 metres in length, with a plain dark grey body and a fairly low dorsal fin. After much debate, we concluded that it was a pilot whale.

Worldwide we currently have about 77 species of cetaceans and of these, 33 are recorded in European seas and 23 occur in British waters.

Of all the whales around our waters the ones we see most commonly are minke, pilot and sometimes orca. The minke has rather unkindly been called by some the "wimpy" whale because it is not very active when swimming and is thought to be a bit "thick". For a long time it was thought to be a plankton feeder, but it is now known that minkes will also eat shoaling fish.

When you observe whales in their true environment, you find yourself puzzled by many questions: Where are they going? How long do they live? How fast can they swim?

In fact, very little is known about the home range of whales (the territory they occupy). Minkes do return to set feeding areas year after year. The orca, or killer whale, on the other hand, can have a territory stretching for over 250 miles and can travel 100 miles in a single day, foraging for food. Studies have now revealed that there are in fact two forms of orca, which have been called "resident" and "transient". Since these names were adopted, it has been found that this does not indicate movement patterns as precisely as once thought, but the names have stuck. However, what is interesting is the fact that the diet of the two groups is different: in general, transient orcas are marine-mammal eaters and resident orcas eat fish, although again, just to be awkward, individuals can vary from the norm sometimes. One thing is certain – orcas are not dangerous to man and no documented cases of them killing a human being has ever been found. Their reputation for man-eating is like that of the wolf or tiger and reflects human encroachment on the animals' territory, overfishing and pollution.

The maximum number of orcas I have ever seen in one pod is six, but they can go around in groups of about 40 individuals. This is very different to the far more gregarious pilot whales who can be found in groups of up to several hundred. What a sight that must be. It is common in these large groups of pilot whales to have smaller groups consisting of one large male with a harem of females and some young males.

Of the small cetaceans, porpoises and different species of dolphin can be seen round about. The common dolphin is the fastest of all the dolphins and can travel at speeds of up to 27 mph. This chatterbox of the sea eats squid, small fish and shrimp. It differs from the bottlenose, which is also found in our waters, mostly in colour, but also in that it cannot stay under water for very long, averaging only about 3 minutes compared to 15 minutes for the bottlenose.

All of these magnificent creatures are perfectly adapted to their environment: they are torpedo-shaped to help with movement through the water; external hind limbs are absent; the front limbs are modified to form flippers but still retain remnants of the five digits of the hand. The animals have no external sexual organs: the penis is hidden and the teats of the female are retracted into slits.

When you watch a whale dive, the arched back disappears and the animal slides gracefully into the deep blue waters. They are obviously well adapted for this internally and oxygen is exchanged via a rich and complicated network of capillaries from the elasticated collapsed lungs. Then you see the arched back surface, and inside the elastic lungs expand, the blowhole plug opens, a cloud of spray is forced up and clean air is taken in again. Quite an amazing process!

And what sophisticated locating equipment the cetaceans have! They need it to locate their prey, as light is absorbed very quickly in water. Only 10 meters down 90% of white light is absorbed. It is not really surprising then that these incredible animals do not rely on their eyes but use another incredible adaptation – echo-location.

A dolphin, for example, will emit a steady beam of sound. Sound can bend and pass through some objects, but the dolphin can judge when it is bouncing off fish. It then turns, emitting clicks at the fish at something like 200 clicks a second. From the returning echoes it can estimate the distance and how long it will take to reach the fish. If you have ever watched the accuracy of a golden eagle plucking a grouse from the moorland, the dolphin does it better and without eyes. And what is even more fascinating is that there is now evidence to suggest that the sounds they emit may stun or even kill the fish prey. Nature is truly a wonderful design engineer.

Although many nations have stopped killing cetaceans, some still continue this barbaric and species-threatening practice even with populations of the larger whales like the sperm and blue whale now at dangerously low levels. As humans we have sought material profit from the whale for generations, procuring the whale flesh and body by blowing its brains out with an exploding harpoon. We could and should seek the deeper spiritual side to these animals – after all, they developed brains of a similar capability to our own 25 million years before us, and they therefore have so much to teach us.

It is not necessary to go to a marine park to see these animals perform in captivity as they are here in their true environment in the coastal waters around our islands. It is far better to observe the large dorsal fin of an orca whale as it breaks the surface in the Minch than to see the animal performing in some degrading aquapark.

Many years ago I was looking at a Neolithic chambered cairn, which had been excavated in the 1930s, at Rubh an Dunain, the peninsula at Glenbrittle on Skye. (The excavation itself has a funny story as the man who did it was forbidden to excavate by the MacLeods of Dunvegan, so he anchored a yacht off the point and worked in the evenings.)

On this particular day, I sat by myself on the top of the cairn and saw a gleaming back and dorsal fin break the surface of the water. The emotional excitement of this cannot really be explained in words. It was a pilot whale alone and heading out to sea.

I came home that evening and sat quietly reading the paper. There, staring me in the face, were pictures of the annual pilot whale slaughter in the Faroes. Of course, I knew that every year "tradition" dictates that these animals are driven aground in a bay where they are hacked to death by butchers with knives. But somehow today it seemed all the more barbaric. Of course, it was not any worse than any other time, but it was just that seeing the whale myself that day had brought it home.

Tradition seems to be the cop out to explain away anything we do which we cannot justify on any moral or other reasonable grounds. "It has to be because it is how we used to do it." At one time cannabalism used to be "tradition" to some tribes. Should we not therefore allow them to carry on their own "tradition"? Of course not, but why then can we justify other equally cruel practices on these grounds? Is it only because they are not inflicted on humans?

I thought of the cairn where I had been sitting that day. It dates from about 4000 BC. What would the world of whales have been like at this time? What would these Neolithic people have experienced in our waters?

They would have found the seas teeming with dolphins, porpoises and whales. Since that time these animals have been destroyed by every means possible. When one species was on the verge of extinction we have gone on to tackle another. The number of cetaceans we have left today in the waters of the world is only a fraction of what would have been around when these Neolithic people roamed the countryside. We now have only one-third the number of cetaceans left as compared with the start of this century. This drastic loss clearly must not be allowed to continue.

While we all criticise the great whaling nations like Japan and Russia the real problem is you and me. Yes, *you and me*, and millions like us, who populate and pollute these creatures' environment. Next time you are near the coast look out to sea and think of the waters full of these incredible animals, all the different species with different songs pulsating through the waters; these sounds have codes locked into them, so detailed they can depict emotion, news, history, happiness and sorrow. And then reflect on what we collectively are doing to the seas.

Chapter 9 ~ Paul

"FOR I AM CONVINCED THAT MAN HAS SUFFERED IN HIS SEPARATION FROM THE SOIL
AND FROM THE OTHER LIVING CREATURES OF THE WORLD."

—GAVIN MAXWELL

No other animal in Britain has such a magnetic attraction as the otter. Much has been written about these wonderful animals, but they were really brought to fame by the well-known author Gavin Maxwell, in his book *Ring of Bright Water*, and later in other books such as Henry Williamson's *Tarka the Otter* and Hugh Miles's *The Track of the Wild Otter*. Gavin's otters were a different species to our own native otters: they were clawless cape otters and his book explains how he reared and tamed these creatures in the wilds of Camusfearna in the North West Highlands of Scotland.

In Britain we have only one native species of otter, the Eurasian otter (Lutra lutra), which can be found from the west coast of Ireland right over into eastern Asia and Japan. This may seem as if they are widespread, but many populations are fragmented and sparse. Indeed, otters are under drastic decline in many parts of Britain and Europe, due totally to human interference, pollution and general lack of respect for the environment. In the North West Highlands, and especially on Skye, we are fortunate to have a healthy population of otters, but we must not become complacent. It is all too easy to lose them.

To see an otter is such a joy. I saw my first one on Skye in June 1980. It was just a quick glimpse as the animal darted along the coastline at Glasnakille, but I got such a tingly feeling in my neck. Even now, having been fortunate to see many, many more otters, I still get this same feeling – a feeling of excitement, of sheer emotional pleasure – but nothing can replace that very first day when I realised the moving piece of brown kelp really was an otter.

Over the years we have learnt so much more about these wildest of wild creatures and grown to love and respect them, but I would like here to tell you about just two of our close encounters.

It was a cold day in January 1986. The ground was frosty and the sun took some of the chill from the northerly wind. We set off for a walk along the shore not far from Broadford, in an area which is a haven for many types of wildlife. Lying on some of the offshore rocks were four common seals, which looked up and then seeing nothing of interest rested their heads back on the seaweed.

As we watched through binoculars, my eye was taken by a short but sudden movement in the water to the right of the seals. Before we could identify the movement the tingling started in my neck and I knew there was an otter about. To our right a head popped up with a blenny in its mouth and the otter swam to a nearby rock where it proceeded to eat the fish. We quickly set up the telescope through which we could identify the animal as our local male nicknamed "Screwface". A few minutes later he was joined by his mate and by two cubs, about the size of rabbits, and the four of them sat on the rocks and groomed and played while we sat on our rocks and watched.

Many authoritative books written about otters often do not give the complete picture. The main population of otters occupy the marine environment, mostly in the north west of Scotland and the Shetland islands. However, most books deal with Eurasian otter populations occurring in rivers in Europe, which often appear to behave in a very different way.

Our own data and observations seem to contradict many of the long-established "facts" about otters. For example, it is said that they are shy, elusive, nocturnal and solitary animals which may be observed early in the morning, late at night and on an ebbing tide. In fact, there is a distinct lack of correlation between sightings of otters and the time of day or tide state, although in a few locations a tidal race may encourage fishing at certain tide states. The otter has no biological adaptations for being nocturnal, although it has very good eyesight, good senses of touch and smell and acute hearing. It is significant that increased nocturnal activity occurs in areas of human population, and it is in these areas where most of the detailed studies of otters are done, even though they do not have the largest populations.

We are also told that they are solitary and that the male has no contact with the cubs. But sitting there on our rocks on that January day, we could see that this too was not necessarily the case. There in front of us we could see the caring behaviour of both mother and father as they settled down to sleep, wrapped around the little cubs to protect them from the chilling wind. Suddenly the animals leapt up obviously alarmed by something which we had not heard and they plopped into the sea water, swimming very fast towards the south and out of sight.

The funny thing about otter watching, which many people find, is that otters have this uncanny way of just simply disappearing, even though you think you are watching carefully. This was one of those occasions and their slim bodies quickly carried them through the water and they vanished.

As always, Nature has done a wonderful job in designing the otter, enabling these animals to live mostly on land but to hunt in the water. Otters do not have a thick insulating layer of blubber like seals do and so their fur is vitally important in heat retention. They spend a lot of time grooming as any loss of condition in the fur can be fatal and this makes them particularly vulnerable to even "minor" pollution events. The otter's fur is much denser than that of a terrestrial mammal and has two layers: an outer layer of long guard hairs and an inner layer of finer denser underfur. The feet have webbing which extends further down the toes than other mammals.

If you watch an otter swimming fast, you will see that they tuck their front feet to the side and move their body up and down like a porpoise for greater speed; at low speeds they will paddle like a dog.

Obviously our otters this day had put on "full speed ahead" and we picked ourselves up from the frozen ground and started on our journey back. As we joined the houses at the road end, I heard a short peeping and we turned back towards the shore. Yes, sure enough, there was our family of otters; the dog otter had gone, but mother was there a long way off shore trying to beckon her young to follow her. We slid down the grassy bank and slowly walked to the shoreline where one cub was obviously defying mother's command. We could see so clearly the parallel with the times of calling our own daughter Kirsty when she would become "deaf", just like this naughty cub.

We sat by the shoreline and the cub sat and watched. With very gentle squeaks I called out and the cub moved closer, then stopped. Her mother called louder so we decided that we should leave and not get the poor creature into any more trouble. From the road we looked back just as the mother came and bit the little rebel on the rump. With a squeal it followed, just like a child will learn to obey after a short smack.

For some time now, the clouds over Beinn na Caillich had been blackening and soon it would be snowing, so we decided that we had better retreat. As we walked, the sky grew still darker and flakes of white fell on the bare landscape turning the shoreline into a white blanket. Two oystercatchers flew over calling "peet-peet" as they went, obviously seeking shelter from the falling snow. A lonesome herring gull cowered on a rocky outcrop not enjoying one bit of it and we returned home to a warm, comfortable house.

We have had many encounters with otters since then, all memorable, but the saddest must surely be Billy.

The summer was a long way behind us and autumn had come in with a vengeance, with rain and cold weather being the norm for most of the past two months. This evening was no exception and the strong wind pushed the rain heavily against the living room window. With every gust the log fire would give out a short roar and burst into life. It was about 10 o'clock when there was a loud knocking on the front door, which instantly sent our collie dog into a frenzy of rapid barking; of course, we were used to this but the more he did it the more annoying it became. "Shut up, Sam," I bellowed loudly as I made my way to the front door.

A rather wet and frantic man stood dripping on the step.

"An otter," he said, "lying on the road. I hit it with the car and I think I've killed it. It just ran out in front of me."

"Grace, Grace," I called. "An injured otter on the road. Get the gloves and I'll fetch the box."

We started the vehicle and followed behind the man's car. The rain was still lashing and soon we stopped in front of a parked car with its lights flashing. There were people crowding around the rather helpless creature, which lay still with blood trickling from its mouth, left paw and tail. Its eyes were closed and its once inquisitive whiskers moved not an inch. But it was breathing and its body moved up and down with slow pants.

We put on our protective gloves and carefully positioned the otter on the blanket, lifting it very gently into the large plastic box which we had used time and time again in our work caring for sick and orphaned seals. It might seem odd putting on gloves to handle an animal which is so lifeless, but many a seemingly calm individual can suddenly come to life when moved and sink its teeth into the nearest unprotected hand.

When we got home Grace examined it very carefully and I made a hasty phone call to our vet. Unfortunately, our own local vet was off sick and a locum had come in to take his place and he was rather reluctant to see or examine the otter. But we went along anyway and when we arrived at the surgery we carefully lifted the box out. The otter seemed to have come around a bit from the stun of the car impact. We told the locum what had happened and about the obvious injuries and he grunted. He asked us to hold the animal firmly while he briefly felt the back left foot, but the otter made no movement. "I don't think it's broken" he snapped. "See how it does overnight."

We reluctantly drove home, with a strong feeling that there is a great lack of interest in care for wildlife. If this had been a valuable highland cow or sheep, possibly more would have been done. It was now after midnight, the rain had eased a little, but the wind was turning to the north west, making it very inhospitable.

In the morning when Grace opened the door to the unit she was confronted with Billy, his two paws on the top of his box as he tried hard to climb out. She was delighted and I entered the room to see her face beaming like a child with a new toy. I took a fish from the fridge and presented it to Billy, who immediately grasped it in both paws and ate it. He muzzled up to the edge of the box again as if to ask for more and we watched thrilled as he ate and ate. We knew we were on a winner. Billy went on improving throughout the day although he still dragged his back paw and we knew this most definitely had to be looked at more closely.

We contacted the vet again who said he would call down if he had time later in the day. We made a "crusher" out of chicken wire and wood which we could place over Billy's cage and push down gently on top of him, so that he could be examined without those sharp canine teeth getting anywhere near our human flesh. The teeth of an otter can cause terrible damage to unwary hands, and in a chapter in Ring of Bright Water,

Gavin Maxwell warns that an otter can bite clean through a hand. After all, if you watch the way they cut straight through fish you will realise that this animal is one to treat with extreme caution.

We had also arranged with the local hospital to X-ray the leg, so all that was needed was an examination by the vet and we could finally treat this animal. When the locum vet arrived he was again very reluctant to examine Billy, which I presume was through lack of experience with wildlife. I say this because we were very disillusioned with the fact that he made no efforts to ascertain what was actually wrong with this animal and was not having anything to do with the X-ray. We were left in a state of turmoil as he still said the leg was not broken, so all we could do was take his word on that account. We longed to have our own vet back who was well accustomed to otters, having been the one who treated Gavin Maxwell's otters at Camusfearna. But we were stuck with this one.

The next day Billy's recovery was even better and he was hobbling around his box. He was inquisitive and starting to be playful and we began to think that maybe we had misjudged the vet and that it would only be time before he would be well again. In one of the large indoor seal tanks we made a platform for Billy's box and filled the rest with water. He could now swim a little, clean himself and haul out into his makeshift holt. All in all he seemed happy and a bond developed between us – a bond of love and friendship between human and animal.

In the evening we planned how we would build a large pen with a pool and keep Billy here until he recovered fully. We had stocked up with some special fish as otters have a different diet to seals, but by the morning things had taken a rather different turn.

It was sunny that morning and we watched from the house window as an otter ran across the far island annoying three oystercatchers on its way. It plopped into the water to start fishing and we watched as it dived and reappeared. On average it stayed down for about 20 seconds before coming up for breath and submerging again. On its tenth attempt it struck lucky and appeared with a large fish in its mouth, which it took to the shore to eat in peace. However, it was constantly annoyed by two herring gulls which bombed it from the air.

We went into the unit and over to Billy's pen. He lay still on the floor. He was breathing very faintly and showed no interest in food. We called the vet.

Grace picked Billy up and his head turned a little but fell back. We had had him for five days, but alas it seemed no more. Within a few minutes he was dead and his poor body lay lifeless in her arms.

We both felt so helpless, conscious of our lack of knowledge.

Billy's body was sent to Inverness for autopsy. He had died of liver problems, which had possibly been brought on by chemical poisoning; he also had badly damaged paws, a broken leg on the left side, a broken jaw and broken toes. Now I am no vet, but a qualified person would surely have been able to identify these problems with a proper examination.

We are now fortunate to know a lot more about otters and how to help them. Our local vet is excellent and can always be counted on for advice and help and we have so many contacts throughout the country whom we can phone that an incident like this will never happen again.

The trouble with working with animals is that you get so involved. You cannot just look and observe and enjoy otters; you want to protect them, do more to understand them and try to find out why these creatures, these ambassadors to the state of our natural environment, are so at risk.

The otter looking down from the very top of the food pyramid sees things we cannot. He watches our environment being destroyed and starved of life; he sees his rivers and the sea being polluted by human negligence, and sadly he dies. And the more otters die, the more the natural world shouts at us to stop. Take away the kings of the different habitats – the lions, the cheetahs, the whales, the eagles and the otters – and our own chances of survival are diminished.

The long-term response needed for the conservation of otters, as well as other species, involves major changes in the outlook of people and governments. And the changes start with you and me.

Chapter 10 ~ Grace

People often ask us how we came to be involved in animal rescue, and in a way, the answer is that we almost seemed to fall into it. I think if you ask the same question of most people who work in this field the answer will be more or less the same – they simply could not stand by and do nothing. Some people have said to us that really we should not interfere as it is just Nature's way of controlling the population by getting rid of the weaker individuals. Nature does indeed control populations very well, which makes rather a nonsense of high-minded human ideas that they will "manage the countryside" or control "potentially high" populations by culling, since they know best.

However, in most cases wildlife casualties are a direct result of human activity: cars, overhead wires, and pet cats are unnatural and potentially lethal hazards to our own native wildlife. So we do have a responsibility to try and right some of the wrongs committed by our own species. Some casualties, of course, are not linked to humans as, for example, the orphaned grey seal pups which are swept off the beaches by gales and high tides. These would be natural mortalities but you cannot treat "man-made" casualties and ignore natural ones. If you are in a position to help you cannot turn your back – it is that simple.

When we first started the Field Centre, people began to bring in odd birds with broken wings and it has grown from there. Many people care about injured animals, and if they find one, they try to think of the most likely person to help. This may be the local RSPCA person, or the vet or even the local police, as I found out when I worked in the police station in Broadford. Once we started the Field Centre, people recognised that we cared about nature in general and so I suppose it followed that we would care about injured wildlife.

This then was our reason for starting, but the real beginnings to our animal hospital are very much more personal. It all started with a family event which usually leads to so much pleasure but for us led to heartbreak.

In April 1988, I found out I was pregnant. We had wanted a second child, and Kirsty was now four, so we were delighted. Off I went for my first clinic and blood tests – all routine and simple.

A couple of weeks later, there was a phone call from the doctor asking me to go back for a second blood test. Apparently the blood test had suggested that there might be a problem, although it could also indicate that I was expecting twins – gulp. There was a strong possibility of twins in our family as my mother is a twin and there are lots of sets of twins on her side. They are supposed to miss a generation and that put me right in line for twins. Yes, we wanted a second child, but we were not certain we wanted another two – especially at one go. Mind you, that was the better option, as the results of the test could also indicate spina bifida.

Back I went, and over the next few days, I began to reconcile myself to the fact that we were probably in for twins. It wouldn't be so bad after all, I thought.

Eventually the results of the test came back and it was not a mistake; there definitely was something picked up by the test. So I was sent for amniocentesis which would give the answer. Any woman who has had an amniocentesis test will know how I felt. It is a test where they insert a needle into the womb to draw off some of the amniotic fluid; this will contain some of the baby's cells and these can be examined for defects such as spina bifida and Down's syndrome. The prospect can be quite terrifying, especially when considering the size of the actual needle required, and the more I thought about it, the worse it became. In reality, although it is not pleasant, it is not as bad as I had imagined it to be. The worst part of it is the mental side: first, I was convinced it was a most horrific process which was really going to hurt; then there was the reason why they were doing it – it could mean there was something wrong with my baby, which is every potential parent's nightmare. In the end, I worked myself up into such a stew that the real thing could not possibly have been as bad as I had expected.

Anyway, I had to go to Raigmore Hospital in Inverness for the amniocentesis and then came the worst part of all – the waiting for the results. By now I knew it was not twins as this would have been seen on the scan, so it could be something really awful. Of course, very occasionally, they miss twins on the scan and I clung to this fact, although, deep down, I knew there was something wrong. There was no way I would admit this, though, and I went on busying myself and pushing this to the back of my mind. Luckily for me, we were well into the season by now, so there was plenty to keep me occupied, but it would all come flooding in when we sat down quietly late at night.

One week went and nothing; two weeks and still nothing. I phoned the doctor and he said he would phone Raigmore and see if the results were there. He phoned back. Yes, they were there, and would Paul and I go to the surgery. This then was it. Expect the worst – if everything was fine, he would have said so on the phone.

Although I did expect the worst, until it was actually confirmed, there was still that glimmer of hope. But no – it was as bad as we feared. The amniocentesis had confirmed neural tube defect. This is another way of saying spina bifida.

One of the moral problems we have now with our fancy technology is the ability to terminate a pregnancy in the case of deformity. In the old days, parents did not know that the baby was deformed until birth, so there really was no choice, but now we do know, and we have to make a decision. Luckily, if you can call it that, we were spared this dilemma. Our baby not only had spina bifida, he or she had anencephaly. This is the worst form of neural tube defect where the skull does not develop properly, exposing the brain and so the child will only live a matter of hours at most. It simply cannot survive.

For us then, there was no decision. It would help no one to continue with the pregnancy. All it would mean was more heartbreak for everyone. Our baby could not possibly live and so we were all better to end it now so that we would all get over it sooner. For me personally, I do not know how I would have coped had it been straightforward spina bifida and I had to decide. I am thankful that I was spared that decision and it was all settled for me.

It was arranged then. I would go to Raigmore on the Thursday and I could come home next day. I will not go into the details, but I think the hardest part is to go through it and not have a baby to take home. At the time, I did not want to know if it was a boy or a girl. It would then be even more of a person to lose. Years later, I regretted that decision and wondered about it. Fortunately, later on, when I was expecting Connaire, I was able to ask the doctor if the records showed what sex the baby had been. I had been certain all through that pregnancy that it was a boy – and yes, I was right.

Everyone was very kind. They always are at times like these. But no one really knows what to say. I found it hard the first time I saw a new baby after that, knowing that ours was dead, but I overcame that and went on.

So what did this have to do with our setting up the animal hospital? As I have said, people had already started to bring us odd casualties they found by the wayside and Paul knew I was interested and wanted to learn more. When he came to collect me from the hospital, he presented me with a book, *First Aid and Care of Wildlife* by Richard Mark Martin. This simple present was the start. It was a brilliant idea. Instead of moping on what had happened I read about what I could do, and this led to a positive attitude which made it so much easier.

That November, at the time when our baby would have been due, I was in Docking at the Greenpeace/RSPCA seal rescue unit and all around me were crying babies (and adults). The phocine distemper virus had arrived and was wiping out thousands of seals, but I will talk more about this in the next chapter. Really though, it was not that different to dealing with human babies – cleaning mess, feeding and plaintive cries. I was glad to be there, and if it had not been for that book, I would probably have been at home fretting about what could, but in reality could never, have been. I have told the full story not only to explain how the animal hospital began, but also hopefully to give some encouragement to those unfortunate enough to find themselves in a similar situation. Everyone has to deal with these things in their own way, but I would simply say that if you lose a child, try and be positive; no matter how shattered you feel, look forward and try again. Deciding to try again is probably the hardest part as, although it seems very unfair, the chances of a deformity occuring again go up, not down. It is necessary to be realistic and be ready to face going through the whole awful experience again, but take heart from those who have gone on and now have wonderful healthy children. We went on and now have two great little boys, Ben and Connaire, as well as Kirsty.

Chapter 11 ~ Grace

"WHAT IS LIFE? IT IS THE FLASH OF A FIREFLY IN THE NIGHT.
IS IT THE BREATH OF A BUFFALO IN THE WINTER TIME?"

—CROWFOOT

To be honest, our knowledge at the beginning of our work in animal rescue was very limited, but we are fortunate in having a great vet nearby. His only drawback is that he has such a vast area to cover that he can be over on the other side of Glenelg when a casualty comes in. However, he is always willing and keen to help and we have learnt a lot from him.

Our facilities, too, were very limited to start with, but gradually we have developed and improved. Small animals can be housed fairly easily, but when we started to take in seals we realised we would need somewhere special for them and for animal rescue in general. We investigated various possibilities and in the end came to the conclusion that a portacabin was the most practical solution.

The portacabin was to be delivered while I was away in Docking learning more about seal care and so I looked forward to returning to the start of a proper animal rescue unit. When I returned home there was the portacabin in all its glory. There was only one snag – it was not where it was supposed to be – beside the house by the burn; it was literally in the driveway and to get in and out to the house you had to take a deep breath and squeeze between it and the gatepost (the gate had already been removed.) Apparently the lorry delivering it could not turn enough to get the portacabin on site and so had just dumped it – and it was well and truly dumped. The only solution was to get a crane to come and lift it, but this would take another four days to arrange.

Eventually the crane arrived to lift the portacabin and swing it into position – beside the house by the burn. Nothing is ever that simple. "Can't do that," said the crane driver, "the gatepost is in the way." So out came the gatepost and a good bit of the fence as well.

Then up went the portacabin and we held our breath as it swung precariously on the end of the long chains. It really was pretty tight and we were more than a little anxious as it swung extremely close to the windows of the end bedroom. But, fortunately the crane driver knew what he was doing and eventually, several nail-bitten minutes later, there was the portacabin at last – beside the house by the burn.

All that remained was for us to cement in the legs and there was our ready-made animal rescue unit. But fate held one last card. That night, before we had a chance to concrete down the legs, there was an almighty gale and there was our precious portacabin rocking dangerously in the wind. There was no alternative but to bring anything and everything which was heavy and plonk it in the portacabin to hold it down. We struggled against the wind with boulders, concrete blocks, and all sorts of things and eventually we felt it was reasonably secure. Fortunately, fate's last card was not a joker and the next day the portacabin was still in place. Needless to say, the concreting was next on the agenda.

That year, 1988, disaster struck the population of common seals around British waters. A vicious virus, later identified as the phocine distemper virus, wiped out thousands of seals; not only British seals but those around the Netherlands and Denmark were also severely affected. In fact, the European seals suffered tremendously with something like 60% dying.

The cause of the virus was debated at great length: some argued that it was a natural way of controlling an increasing population of common seals; others insisted that it was caused by pollution, as the worst hit areas were in the North Sea and Wadden Sea, both well known for their high pollution levels. In a way I feel that the answer lies in between, and this is not because I want to sit on the fence. Yes, I agree viruses are naturally occurring organisms and, indeed, epidemics do break out from time to time, but there is no denying the fact that the seals at greatest risk were in the most heavily polluted areas. Human colds are also naturally occurring viruses but if you work and live in a healthy environment, you are more likely to be able to fight them off than if you are in a dirty, polluted environment. The same would seem true for the seals: the virus did occur naturally, but the seals in the North and Wadden seas were already run down because of the pollution levels and were therefore more susceptible to it.

Although, on this basis we could hope to be more fortunate with our own seals, as our waters on the west coast are relatively clean, we knew that if anyone was going to receive sick seals on Skye, it would be us. Seals were a whole different ball game to the casualties we had already encountered and so we felt that we must equip ourselves with as much knowledge and experience as possible beforehand.

We had already had advice on rearing seal pups from Laurance Larmour of the Sea Life Centre near Oban, who had been rearing orphaned seals for several years. So when I went to the Greenpeace/RSPCA unit at Docking, I did have a very limited knowledge of seal treatment, but not of the virus. At the time I was there, they had 27 seals indoors and 4 in the pools outside. They were mostly adult common seals with differing degrees of the virus but also a few grey seal pups. Indoors each seal was housed in an isolation tank, closely resembling a gigantic mixing bowl. Some had to be tube-fed, others were force-fed whole fish and a few were feeding themselves.

The importance of real dedication to the job was brought home to me in one small but unforgettable incident. There was one particular grey seal pup called Bilbo, who was not at all friendly. In fact, he really was a bit vicious and difficult to handle. He was still being tube-fed, which involved one person sitting astride him and the other gently putting the tube down, taking care not to get it down the windpipe, and then pouring down the delicious, smelly fish soup. One afternoon, Bilbo was not in a particularly good mood, and he was due to be fed by an RSPCA inspector, whom I will call Michael. Michael did not appear to have any love for animals. In fact, I do not think he even liked them, so why he went for that particular career I cannot imagine. Anyway, Michael went into the tank with Bilbo. "Right you b★★★★★★, I'm going to get you" – not the best way to win the confidence of a nervous animal, let alone a wild animal, which is not used to human contact of any kind. The more he tried to "get" Bilbo, the more reluctant Bilbo became. The swearing got worse and eventually after a lot of wrestling Michael yelled "Right you little s★★★, you can b★★★★★ well starve". And at that he stamped out of the tank and left Bilbo wondering what had hit him.

A few minutes later, a volunteer called Ian came along and asked what was wrong with Bilbo. I explained what had just happened, and I shall not record his reply, but needless to say he was not impressed! He left Bilbo alone to calm down for half an hour and then stepped quietly into the tank with him. Bilbo flew at him, but Ian stayed perfectly still and quiet. The seal began to relax and then Ian gently lowered himself on to him and the feeding was over in a few seconds.

Of course, I do not believe Bilbo understood what was being said to him, but he 'read' exactly what was meant through the manner and the aggression of Michael. Ian, on the other hand, treated him calmly but firmly and the animal reacted positively to it. What really got me was that Michael was earning a good living "looking after animals", while Ian had given his time as a volunteer to help if he could and he would shortly have to leave to go back to work to try and earn a living. Fortunately, I know that Michael is not typical of RSPCA inspectors and many are working away looking after animals in a truly caring and efficient way, but there are also those whose suitability to the job has to be seriously questioned.

Also while I was away in Docking, four seals came in to Paul, so for him it was in at the deep end. They did not have the virus but were orphaned grey seal pups. Two of them came over from Uist (At first the ferrymen were a bit perplexed to find seals coming over by boat – why couldn't they swim themselves? – but now they are used to it.) The third pup came from Durness and became known as "Fatty Uwe" as she quickly began feeding herself and had such an insatiable appetite that she seemed to swell like a balloon.

The fourth pup came from Skye, in fact, he was found in the middle of the Sleat road near Kinloch. We have a habit of not naming seals after their finders and so this one became known, strangely enough, as "Kinloch".

Right from the start Kinloch was "different" and he made his presence well known. When Paul received the phone call telling him about the seal pup in the middle of the road, he was discussing potential Duke of Edinburgh Award expeditions on Skye. Simon, who had come to sort out these things, agreed to go with him to collect the seal, so, armed with a big box, they set off down to Sleat. There in the middle of the road lay the most pathetic looking seal pup – not the usual fluffy white cuddly-looking little creature, but a dirty, wet, grimy, skinny little mess, but still with the appealing black eyes.

Paul and Simon scooped him up into the box and set off back to Broadford. Suddenly Paul glanced into his rear view mirror and saw an extra passenger sitting on the seats – sitting up and peering out of the windows was Kinloch, who had somehow managed to clamber out of his box. Then as quickly as he had appeared he vanished, and seconds later his head appeared between Simon's legs, snapping at his feet. You can imagine the scene as Paul tried to keep his eyes on the road until the next passing place would allow him to stop and recapture the runaway while Simon sat with his feet on the dashboard trying to avoid the snapping teeth. What seemed like an age later the Landrover stopped and a relieved Simon flew out the passenger door. Kinloch was replaced in his box and the rest of the journey passed without further escapes. I doubt if Simon will ever forget his visit to Skye and his close encounter of the flippered kind.

During my stay in Docking, I would phone home every evening with the latest tips I had learnt. At this time Trish used to work with us and, with her help and that of a few loyal volunteers, Paul kept the seals fed and cleaned.

By the time I returned they were experts and they had the routine of feeding and cleaning well sorted. The first three seals were coming on well, but Kinloch was a real problem. He really could not stand humans. All wild animals have a fear and dread of humans, which is quite natural when you consider how badly we often treat them, but some find it even more difficult to accept us. All seals will bite, which can be very disconcerting when they look so innocent; but every time anyone went near Kinloch he would fly at them and sink his teeth into whichever bit he could reach. Poor Martin, who has spent so much time helping us with the animals, has a nasty scar on his arm to remind him of Kinloch.

One thing we have found is that seals often adopt one person as their mother-figure; you do not choose the seal, it chooses you, and its "mother" can handle it far easier than anyone else. The funny thing was that Kinloch chose me and although he still was not easy to handle he did not seem quite as vicious with me. It is not that I can claim the credit or that I treated him any differently (I wish I had, because then I would know how to do it again!) But whatever it was, it ended up that Kinloch became known as my seal and I nearly always held him for feeding.

The other three seals were flourishing, feeding themselves and putting on weight quickly. But not my poor Kinloch. He looked as pathetic as the day he came in. No matter how much food we gave him, he never put on any weight and each feed was a traumatic experience for him.

By now, the oil rig Buchan Alpha had donated an old life raft which served as a temporary pool for the seals. The first three loved it, but not Kinloch – he seemed to hate water. Often grey pups are afraid of the pool until they are feeding themselves, and that is fairly natural when you realise that they do not go into the water until they have been left on their own by their mothers and are ready to feed themselves. Until that time they stay above high water and wait for Mum to feed them.

Sadly, Kinloch never overcame his troubles and one day in January we found him dead beside the pool. We often wondered how he had come to be at Kinloch as there are no grey seal pupping areas on the main part of Skye and certainly nowhere near Sleat. All we can imagine is that someone found him and took him home, only to find him too much of a handful, so they just threw him out again. This is one of the problems with seal pups: they are so lovable and lost-looking that well-meaning people think they must do something to help. Often this is not the right thing to do, and so we always advise people to leave well alone for at least 24 hours, provided, of course, the pup is not sick or injured or in any imminent danger. Hopefully during that time the mother will return, since she will do a much better job of rearing her young one than we can and we must always give her the chance before stepping in to help.

Kinloch was not the only seal to escape. In fact, seals seem to have a real streak of Houdini in them. On one occasion Paul had gone up to meet the ferry for a pup. It is nice to be welcomed, but he was definitely unnerved when greeted by the ferryman with, "Thank God you're here." Apparently, a seal had escaped in the back of a lorry on the ferry and no one would dare go near him. Armed with a pair of strong gloves Paul soon had the captive in a box (by now we had invested in a high-sided box from which they could not escape!)

Seals have characters as various as humans – some are awkward and unfriendly like Kinloch and some are just dying to be loved. One such lovable and loving creature was tiny Rhu, a little common seal sent over from Uist. She had been found on a beach and still had part of her umbilical cord attached. Unfortunately, the message "leaving them alone" had not got through to the well-intentioned people who picked her up, and the first we heard of it was that she was in the kitchen of the house in which they were staying on holiday. By this time there is no point putting a young animal back as the mother will almost certainly reject it.

So little Rhu came over on the ferry. She was tiny, just like a little cat and she longed for love. Although we obviously do not want to humanise any of our wildlife casualties they still need affection and care, especially the young ones. But Rhu seemed to need loving contact more than most, perhaps because of her young age. Every look from those huge appealing eyes seemed to say "Love me" and we all did. She seemed to be doing well to begin with, but then she suddenly took a turn for the worst and we lost her. We feel the loss of all our casualties but losing little ones like this seem to be worse.

Sometimes the seals present us with challenges beyond "simply rearing them" – although, of course, this is not a simple process. Over the late autumn and winter of 1991 we received eight seals; five were orphaned grey seal pups and four of these responded well to treatment. However, the fifth, Sally, did present us with a few headaches. Because she was the smallest one we had at the time, she was picked on by the big ones, and in the end she became so fed up with it she went completely off her food and started losing weight again. So she had to be taken back into the unit and kept there for a little while until the big boys had been put back to the wild. Then, just as she was starting to put on weight again, she developed a prolapse, which was not a condition we had encountered before. To us, such a condition would be pretty disastrous, but it is wonderful what nature can overcome. With the aid of our vet and a visiting locum, the condition was treated, she began to thrive and there was an extra-special thrill in releasing her one cold Sunday morning in January.

The problems between Sally and the bigger seal pups only served to reinforce our resolve to get a second larger seal pool adjacent to the existing one. We had already felt that this was necessary to provide better facilities for patients, but it was now obvious to us that we needed to be able to separate aggressive seals from smaller ones, when both need access to pool facilities.

The remaining three seals from that winter had quite serious injuries. Cara, an older grey seal pup came in with a severe injury to her eye. At first it looked as if she would lose this eye altogether but to everyone's delight it gradually began to recover, responding wonderfully to homeopathic treatment. From time to time we have seen seals in the wild which are either blind in one eye or totally blind. They seem to survive quite happily and manage to feed by using their whiskers to sense the movement of the fish in the water and now it is also believed that seals use a form of echo-location to find prey. Fortunately for Cara, though, she was soon able to use both eyes again.

The other two seals had wounds caused by rope and netting. One was a common seal of about six months, which we found on Christmas Eve just outside Broadford. Fortunately, her wounds were not too severe and, after a few days rest, she was able to be released again. The other seal was not so lucky. She had been found on Uist with a vicious gash right round her neck where she was caught fast in rope. A friend from Uist, who rescued her, painstakingly cut her free and cleaned up the wound and two days later she came across to us on the ferry. Although the wound still looked nasty, it was clean and began to heal. She went out to the pool where she loved the water and things seemed to be going well. But then suddenly she seemed to give up. It is tragic when this happens: if an animal gives up the will to live, there is nothing you can do.

These last two seals unfortunately suffered like so much of our marine life from the debris of rope and loose netting thrown overboard from boats. How many times have we walked along a beautiful Skye beach and picked our way carefully over the seaweed covered stones and through the plastic rubbish and nylon rope. It is obviously an eyesore to humans, and many visitors to our island have commented on it, but it can be lethal to animals and birds, both wild and domestic: I have seen cows choking on the rope which for some peculiar reason they have tried to eat; we have had many seabirds with their beaks entwined in the evil nylon threads; and our seals were caught in pieces of normal fishing net. All too often it is too late to help and the unfortunate creature dies either from its injuries or drowns in the underwater nets. We are now all familiar with the pictures of dolphins and seals caught in nearly invisible drift nets, but clearly these pieces of rope and ordinary netting can be equally lethal.

Cleaning beaches removes the unsightly mound of rubbish, but it does not cure the problem as it all comes flooding back with the next storm and with it comes a feeling of futility as the beach returns to its former plastic-strewn condition. We are only treating the symptom and not the disease. We really have to treat the problem at source and that is to stop the rubbish from being thrown away in the first place.

We all treat the sea like a giant dustbin. If you throw rubbish on the floor, it stays there and is obvious, but if you throw it into the sea, it vanishes and therefore it is gone, even though it will reappear one day to decorate some distant shore. The same goes for liquid waste – you would not get away with pouring sludge all over the ground even in some remote highland glen. But pour it into the sea and it is absorbed and disappears as if into some great magical sponge.

The majority of us do not really consider the problem of waste. We throw rubbish into the bin and it is collected and goes away. But how many of us actually ask where it goes? All we are concerned about is that it goes away from here. Yes, now we are far more conscientious about recycling, but again that does not go far enough. We really must reduce the amount of materials used in the first place if we are going to have any sort of impact on saving energy and conservation in general.

And this is so important if we are to have any long-term success with animal rescue. There is no point rearing seals and caring for them until they are ready to go if we just release them into a cocktail of sludge, chemical waste and bits of plastic and nylon. If we think anything of our casualties, we must ensure that they are able to return to a healthy environment to live out their true wild lives in safety. But we will return to this subject later, as it is not just the seals who suffer from human mismanagement of the environment.

Anyone who finds themselves in a similar situation can contact SATFA (Support After Termination For Abnormality), 73 Charlotte Street, London W1P 1LB (Helpline 0171 631 0285).

Chapter 12 ~ Paul

Our portacabin has proved to be so much more than just a seal treatment unit and is vital for all our animal rescue work. Even the tanks, which were originally designed with seals in mind, have been used for anything and everything. Their great advantage is that they can be hosed down, which makes cleaning so much easier and more thorough. So now the unit contains an assortment of tanks, cages and boxes of various sizes with especially heated ones designed for intensive care; and in the corner is a special shower unit, which was kindly donated by the League Against Cruel Sports, for the treatment of oiled birds.

We are all familiar with the pathetic sight of oiled birds, having seen countless television pictures of the disastrous events in Alaska and the Gulf and most recently Shetland in January 1993. However, it is just another case of wildlife having to suffer because of what we humans want. Every one of us, and there are no exceptions, uses oil; most of us have a car, or go on a bus, or uses plastics (produced from oil), or use electricity (some from oil-fired power stations). It is actually amazing the number of uses for oil apart from the obvious use as a fuel.

We are not saying that we should not use all these things. Technology used carefully and properly can be beneficial to all life, but there is so much waste. How often do we just leap in the car rather than walking to the shops. Do we even give it a thought? Do we ever use public transport rather than using our own private car? It is far more efficient in terms of energy consumption. Obviously, I am not saying that these simple measures are going to stop birds becoming oiled, but a little thought will reduce waste and that can only be of benefit to the environment in general.

A major oil spill leaves a lasting impression of disaster and misery. I was unfortunate enough to go to Shetland as part of the team from the European Wildlife Rehabilitation Association, and while I was there I wrote the following article for the press. I leave it unchanged as it reflects my own thoughts at the time and it will hopefully give you some insight as to what an oil spill is really like.

Eighty-mile-an-hour winds lashed Shetland and the Braer *catastrophe was rapidly becoming a nightmare. With oil appearing on both sides of the island, there is now little hope of containing it.*

It is a sad fact that, in spite of all our fancy technology, the ultimate outcome of whether an oil spill becomes an environmental disaster or not depends more on the forces of nature than man's ingenuity.

These disasters are starting to occur on a rather regular basis: in 1978, the Amoco Cadiz *put 68 million gallons into the sea off Brittany; in 1989, the* Exon Valdez *spewed 11 million gallons onto the Alaskan coast; in December 1992, the* Aegean Sea *deposited 16 million gallons onto Spain. And now the* Braer *— who knows how much has already been spilled and how much is yet to come? Man's greed for consumable hydrocarbons make these spills inevitable.*

The situation on my arrival in Shetland was grim. The airport had the look of a major press extravaganza with representatives from all parts of the world.

We set off for Quendale Bay to see the stricken tanker for ourselves. However, this was not just a disaster of the shoreline — yesterday a Force 12 gale hit the islands and pushed the oil half a mile inland contaminating grass, sheep and water. The roads were covered with greasy oil which splashed up onto our vehicle and the windscreen was smeared with a film of oil which made visibility almost impossible. We drove down a rough track to the bay and the stench was overpowering; my eyes hurt with the fumes, and I was left with a terrible taste in my mouth, which has never gone away.

The ground was covered in a thin film of oil and the grass was nearly dead with small pools of water topped with an oily cocktail. We walked towards the boat as snow lashed into our face and there it was — the Braer. *So close you could almost touch it. A brown "gunge" billowed from below mixed with seawater which was then lashed onto the rocks. It seems incredible but the boat* did not look significantly large and yet the damage it was doing to the environment on Shetland was catastrophic. Fifteen seals swam helplessly in the bay as two corpses floated on the brown waves. Shags covered in oil from head to tail flapped their wings on the rocks with an aimless repetition and helicopters hovered overhead bringing dignitaries and press to look but not do anything about Britain's worst oil disaster.

We were there ourselves on Shetland as part of the European Wildlife Rehabilitation Association (EWRA) team and our task was to set up wildlife rehabilitation facilities in the northern part of the island to treat otters. We were under the supervision of Dr John Lewis of the International Zoo Vet team. Already Pieterburen Seal Rescue had arrived and were busy organising the seal rehabilitation side and the SSPCA were looking for the birds.

Conditions at the start were primitive as we set to producing an animal hospital out of an old tweed factory, which was cold, damp and leaking. Medical supplies had already been flown in, so in two days, with a lot of local islander help, we prepared the building to treat oiled otters with intensive care units, cages, oil cleaning facilities, operating table and long-term enclosures.

The obvious effect of oil spills on wildlife is devastating; they suffer not just from the obvious oil coating but by ingestion of the oil which causes ulceration to the stomach, lung damage and a host of other medical conditions.

Another problem affecting the birds and animals is the inhalation of the fumes given off by the hydrocarbons. Seals, for example, barely lift their nostrils above the surface of the water when they breathe, so as a seal inhales it is likely to breathe in a concentrated dose of these nasty vapours causing the potentially toxic effects of solvent abuse.

Shetland has, or should I say had, a population of between 700 and 900 otters, some 4800 common seals, 3500 grey seals, not to mention the vast seabird colonies. The waters around Shetland are used by common porpoise, white-sided dolphins, white-beaked dolphins, Risso's dolphins and pilot whales. The enormous scale of the disaster is hard to comprehend because many will die at sea and therefore not be counted.

As I write, 90-mile-an-hour winds are due to hit the island, pushing the oil further north to contaminate all of the west coast. Already small amounts contaminate the east so that the whole Shetland coastline may soon be oiled.

This disaster could very easily have been on the west coast of Scotland – in fact, the chances of this happening are highly likely given the fact that the Minch is even more treacherous than the waters around Shetland.

The Braer was a small tanker with some 80,000 tons of oil. Many of the larger super-tankers carry 240,000 tons. The Shetland islands' fishing, fishfarming, crofting and tourism will be severely damaged for many years to come, taking the very heart out of the community and its economy.

The operation of cleaning up Shetland will last a long time but the media interest will soon wane. However, we must not allow ourselves to drift on with the current situation of these supertankers passing through the Minch. The Shetland disaster has focussed attention on the threat to the Minch with its narrow channel of treacherous waters. It is time for everyone — fishermen, fishfarmers, crofters, those involved in the tourist industry and conservationists — to get together to stop the oil tanker activity in the Minch. With 1 billion tons of crude oil per day travelling the world's oceans, a disaster in the Minch is just waiting to happen.

Living on Skye, I see similarities in the countryside and way of life with that on Shetland and it saddens me to see this total destruction of what were such beautiful islands. I would deeply hate to see the nightmare again which I have experienced here.

Oiled birds come in not only because of a major spill such as this, but often because a ship has been carelessly cleaning its tanks; birds can also become oiled because someone dumps the used oil they have changed from the car.

Other chemicals are equally dangerous, such as paint, where the lid has been left off, and we even had a recently fledged dunnock whose tail was covered in cement. Such events can usually be avoided, although in certain circumstances it is difficult to prevent animals and birds from landing where they should not, as in the case of the dunnock.

Acts of deliberate cruelty make us totally enraged: one night in January we had a sudden power cut for several hours. The reason? A Greenland white fronted goose had flown into power lines. This is surely an accident and you could hardly say that the electric company were cruel for putting the power lines there. No, of course not, but I have no hesitation in saying that of the person who set the gin trap which caught the goose's leg, which therefore weakened it and made it unable to fly properly dragging the horrific weight around on its badly torn leg. There was nothing we could do for that unfortunate bird and in a way perhaps it was the kindest thing that it did fly into the wires and die there and then, rather than struggle around for goodness knows how long until it died in agony. The newspapers said that the trap was illegal but had obviously been set for something else – probably a fox – but is that an excuse? Such acts of barbarism are inexcusable.

Poisoning is no better. Again the excuse is that it is set for "vermin" although sometimes there are cases where other creatures are affected, such as pet dogs. It is, of course, tragic if you lose a pet, particularly by such a disgusting act, but is it right that a fox should be writhing in agony from the poison rather than our own dear Fido? Poisoning is a terrible way to die and we had a case where several cormorants died in convulsions after being poisoned.

Road traffic accidents are somewhat different and are generally not a deliberately cruel act. Sometimes it is impossible to avoid an animal or bird which suddenly comes from nowhere and appears just feet from your car. But then, any caring person would stop to see if there is anything they can do to help. Unfortunately, this does not always happen.

One September a group of young walkers brought a tawny owl which had been hit by a car near Inverinate. They had been in the car behind and saw the accident, but the driver just went on unconcerned. They stopped, picked up the bird, which looked as if it was almost dead, and brought it on to us in Broadford. Their caring action saved the bird's life.

Things certainly did not look too good when it arrived, but it did not seem to have any broken bones. However, we have often found that these are not the main problem but rather internal injuries which are more difficult to detect. As it recovered we found that it would hang its head on one side and seemed to be generally "lop-sided". This is often a symptom of concussion and this proved to be the case. Initially he had to be force-fed and he had a very disconcerting habit of keeling over at the end of his feed and looking dead. Five minutes later he would be sitting up again with his head on one side. As time went on he started to tuck into his own food and eventually he was released in some woodland nearby.

Another road casualty was a beautiful sparrowhawk, who taught us in no uncertain terms how we must always take care when handling wildlife. Our patients are frightened, in pain and in an alien environment, so you cannot blame them for defending themselves. This sparrowhawk had a broken wing, which was being examined when it sunk its talons into Grace's hand, which she had carelessly left within reach. I carefully removed the talons, which fortunately had not caused any serious injury. The problem was my lack of spare hands. As I removed one talon and went on to the next, the first would just spring back. I could not hold them out and remove the rest at the same time. Slowly I began to make progress and just as Grace relaxed when I prised off the last one — wham! — In went the other leg with the talons and we had to start again. It was not the sharpness of the talons which literally made an impression on Grace, but the incredible power and force which the bird could exert. (No wonder talons make such an effective killing machine.) Needless to say, we will never forget that sparrowhawk and will always have the utmost respect for any bird of prey and its talons!

Looking back, you do see the funny side of some incidents. I can remember one fine summer's day in July when a lady from Staffin rang saying she had an otter in her byre and it looked scared. Would I come up and see what was wrong? Grace was away in Switzerland with a group and so I put young Ben in the minibus and made the long drive north. When I arrived she pointed me to the byre and armed with strong gloves and a grasper I entered only to hear the door slam shut behind me and the key turn firmly. Now to be perfectly honest, I am quite a nervous character when it comes to handling wildlife. I love and respect wild animals, but that does not mean I really want to be bitten by one. An otter, as I am sure you are all aware, is quite ferocious with a tremendous bite and the thought of having an otter clamped to my hand did not really appeal.

I spent what must have been 20 minutes looking for this creature in the gloom, but hunt as I may, I could not find it. I was beginning to give up hope when I noticed a wheelbarrow sitting on its own, full of slates. I peered underneath some tiles to see an otter cowering and looking distressed. Little did he know that I was also cowering and looking distressed on the other side. I positioned my cage under the barrow, opened one wire door and then proceeded to take away the tiles. One by one I moved them as the otter became more and more obvious and then with about four tiles to go, it leapt out of the barrow and landed in the cage. A quick movement and the cage was closed, followed by a long sigh of relief.

The lady of the house was having quite extensive repairs done and when I banged on the byre door it was opened cautiously by a builder. Outside more builders had gathered and people crowded around to look at the poor sick animal in the wire cage. As I tried to make a quick retreat to give it some peace, one man asked if it was difficult to catch. "A little," I replied, "but with experience it comes easy." I could not believe what I was saying.

Cats are yet another hazard which has to be faced by small birds and animals and like many rehabilitation centres we have received many sad and shocked individuals. Originally, like many people, we felt that the reason we lost quite a few was that they suffered so severely from shock. Of course, it must be an extremely shocking experience to suddenly find yourself pounced upon by a massive set of claws and teeth. However, later on we learnt that although shock is an important factor, death is more likely to be caused by infection through the cat's claws; if this is immediately treated with antibiotics, the chances of survival increase considerably.

The first chance we had to try this out was with a tiny wood mouse which had been caught by a friend's cat. The mouse also had a broken leg but the priority was to give it a shot of antibiotics. Unfortunately, when we looked through our supply of needles, we found that even the smallest was thicker than the mouse's leg, so we clearly needed something smaller. We phoned the surgery and asked if they had any very small needles.

"What is it for?" they asked. "For injecting a mouse," I replied. "OK, fine, come and get it"; so off I went.

When I arrived, I was met with a very quizzical look and the question "What did you say it was for?" "For injecting a mouse," I replied, only to be met with howls of laughter. "Typical, here we all are trying to get rid of mice and you are trying to inject them!"

Amidst lots of giggles, they let us have the needle and to our delight the mouse not only survived but the leg healed well and it soon went on its way. For reasons of neighbourly relations though we felt it best to release it a long way from houses!

We have also received our fair share of young birds and mammals and it is comical to be met by the ever-open mouths of baby birds. Mind you, it does mean a lot of work to try and feed these insatiable appetites.

But it is not only the babies who sometimes do not fly, and not just for reasons of broken wings. From time to time we have received birds which seem perfectly healthy but yet will not fly. We received two of these reluctant fliers on the same day: one, a lesser black-backed gull, came from Dunvegan, and the other was a gannet from the car park at the Sligachan Hotel. Neither had a broken wing and there appeared to be no reason for their being grounded; it was suggested, however, that maybe the gannet had had one too many at the hotel!

After a few days rest and food, the gannet was trying its wings again and appeared well enough to be released – so off it went. The gull though was clearly enjoying its stay and although every day we tried throwing him into the air to launch him, he just flapped his wings pathetically and came back down to earth with a bump. This became a daily ritual which Kirsty found highly amusing, but one day as I was watching their antics from the window, there was great excitement as the gull suddenly seemed to remember what was expected from him and flew off.

I think the easiest "casualties" we receive regularly are the Manx shearwaters. They are not true casualties as there is nothing wrong with them apart from a little confusion and exhaustion. On the nearby Small Isles, Manx shearwaters breed by the thousand – in fact there are 150,000 pairs on the Isle of Rhum. These birds nest in burrows on the hillside and it is an amazing experience to hear the unearthly scream of the birds as they try to locate their mates in the burrows when they return at night with food. Because these burrows are on a slope, it is easy for them to launch themselves into the air without any effort. In the autumn these gentle-looking birds migrate all the way to South America, but if the weather at this time is wet and windy, this is when the trouble starts; young birds become tired and decide to rest on the wet road thinking it is water. They then fall easy prey to cats and run the risk of being run over by cars. So for about two weeks in September, if it is a wet and foul night, we go on "shearwater hunts" to try to find these poor birds. Unfortunately, if it is a beautiful clear starry night they do not land – only on the really awful ones! All you need to do is put the bird into a box, keep it quiet overnight and then in the morning release it over the water. We usually launch them from the pier, but there is no problem if they land on the water as they can manage to take off from there. We are curious though because if they have to travel all the way to South America and they go wrong in Broadford it does not inspire a lot of confidence!

Occasionally we receive other oceanic birds which, like the Manx shearwaters, only really need a rest before being released again. Amongst these, we have had Leach's petrel and a little auk, but these are not common.

Some of the rarities sometimes cause a bit of confusion with identification and quite often we are given a mistaken identity for the patient coming in. However, there was one unforgettable example of this which gives hope to anyone having difficulty identifying birds.

One afternoon, we received a phone call from Kyle. It was from a couple up on holiday who had found a bird with an injured wing. They were not sure what it was but said it had a "red neck". A red-throated diver or possibly a red-breasted merganser sprang to mind, but we said just to bring it in and we would see what we could do. About an hour later they appeared on the doorstep with a small basket covered in a tea-towel. That intrigued me as the basket was so small that if it had contained either a diver or a merganser, we should have been able to see bits of feathers sticking out. But there was nothing. What could it be? So we went into the unit and they gently handed me the basket. With more than a bit of curiosity I lifted the tea-towel, only to be confronted with — a robin!

All these creatures have been treated within our portacabin, but the catalogue of difficulties was not confined to siting the building in the first place. In 1992, the planning officer, who had allowed us to put the portacabin on site during the height of the seal virus, told us to remove it. This presented a major problem, not least the physical problem of actually getting it out, considering the difficulties of getting it in!

However, more important than that is, where do we treat the casualties? Without the portacabin, we would have nowhere to put them, so a solution had to be found. The best answer seemed to be to convert the existing museum building into a specially designed animal hospital with information room and a classroom upstairs. Unfortunately though, this has meant that we have had to postpone building the new seal pool, but that will come some day.

Fortunately, we believe the number of people who care greatly outnumber those who do not. Most of our casualties are brought in by this caring majority — some, as in the case of a lapwing with a badly damaged leg, just leave a box on the doorstep, but they have cared enough to bring it; others care by helping to provide blankets, bowls and free fish; others care by helping out practically with the cleaning and feeding of the animals; and yet others help by providing financial support. Without the help of all these people, no animals would be saved, so we cannot say a big enough thank you to you all.

Chapter 13 ~ Paul

'THE MURDER BUSINESS AND SPORT BY SAINT AND SINNER ALIKE HAS BEEN PUSHED RUTHLESSLY, MERRILY ON, UNTIL AT LAST PROTECTIVE MEASURES ARE BEING CALLED FOR, PARTLY, I SUPPOSE, BECAUSE THE PLEASURE OF KILLING IS IN DANGER OF BEING LOST FROM THERE BEING LITTLE OR NOTHING LEFT TO KILL, AND PARTLY, LET US HOPE, FROM A DIM GLIMMERING RECOGNITION OF THE RIGHTS OF ANIMALS AND THEIR KINSHIP TO OURSELVES'

—JOHN MUIR

Over the years of caring for injured wildlife, we have come to realise that there really is more to it than just caring for the individual animal or bird. Humans generally inflictsome pretty horrendous injuries on animals and the sad fact is that, although many are genuine "accidents", many are sadistically calculated injuries.

We can care for an injured seal but we also have to know that we are putting it back into a relatively safe environment; unless we back this hands-on care with hands-on campaigning, we are losing a time-consuming and emotionally taxing battle. Caring for the helpless little creature we are holding has to go hand in hand with trying to do something to stop the destruction of our native wildlife and its environment.

We may jump up and down about the rainforests or the destruction of the African elephant; we may complain about the Greeks trapping small birds; and yet we allow our taxes to be used to fund the cold-blooded, barbaric destruction of the fox. We are a nation which likes to think we are caring, animal-lovers but we have split ideals. We may give £15 to a conservation charity, thinking we have done our bit and then we bury our heads in the sand to the dangers threatening most of our wildlife heritage.

Campaigning for wildlife protection can and often does have its rather adverse side effects, and the more we get involved, the deeper in trouble we become. But it is like animal rescue itself – we must do something.

Over the years we have launched many campaigns to give British wildlife full protection:

we have campaigned for the seal, the dolphin, the whale and the fox. As we battle away at campaigning, it is interesting to see how little people know about wildlife protection in our own country and in reality how little protection there actually is. If we take the Conservation of Seals Act, for example, in fact this does very little to actually protect seals in the wild although the majority of people believe this to be its purpose.

Nearly everyone likes seals, whether it is the common seal or the grey Atlantic seal, and yet they have no proper legal protection. In Scotland, the threat of a new seal cull is always being bantered about by the fisheries, although it could be argued that in any case an unofficial cull has been carried out by the fishing industry since the early 1980s. Our own research in 1989 put the figure at 6000 seals a year being shot by the fisheries industry and recent evidence supports this figure.

The recently published government figures on seal populations gives the total population of grey seals around the British coast as 93,500. The state of the common seal population is still unclear as the population in England was reduced by 50% in 1988 as a result of the phocine distemper virus, but it is estimated to be about 24,640 in Britain.

We maintain that although grey seal populations have undoubtedly increased, there is a good reason for this and we only have to look back less than 100 years to find this reason. In the nineteenth century, seals were hunted for subsistence, but this was then replaced by commercial hunting for skins. So by 1914, the British population of grey seals had been reduced to the disastrous number of 500 and it was felt necessary to introduce legislation to protect them. This led to the Grey Seals Protection Act of 1914, which was amended in 1970 to include common seals in the Conservation of Seals Act. Is it therefore such a surprise that, when a population had been so seriously attacked, after this pressure was removed it started to bounce back? It may continue to increase for a while, but it will eventually become stable and reach a sustainable level.

We can sympathise with the frustration of the salmon netsman or fishfarmer who feels he is losing a large part of his catch to seals, but where were his anti-predation nets? These are secondary nets outside the inner ones which are designed to keep seals out.

Around our Scottish waters, we have countless fishfarmers who say they have to shoot seals to keep them away from their stock. Some use predation nets but many do not. All in all, the easy and cheapest solution is to shoot any seal which comes nearby, even if it is not actually doing any damage. No one can deny that seals will cause a lot of damage, but all that happens is that one seal is shot and is followed by another and another and another. A long-term solution is not only in the seals' interest but also in the interests of the fishermen or fishfarmer, who then no longer keep losing their stock.

Whilst it is claimed that fishfarmers and netsmen only shoot seals when near the nets, we know for a fact that many fishfarmers will actively go and seek out seals to kill, even attacking them on colonies when they pose no threat. I have personally seen marksmen out at a colony whistle to the seals to attract them and then blast their heads off when they came up to investigate the noise. Seals are inquisitive animals and do respond to whistles, and the idea of using this innocent curiosity as a means of drawing them to the slaughter when they are doing no damage is indefensible. I can find no words to describe the sort of mentality which allows people to act in this way. So do not be conned – seals are dying now just to provide cheap salmon and we can all do something to stop this. The only way to make any impression on these people is to hit them where it hurts – in the bank balance – and we are all able to exert consumer pressure on the market by refusing to buy farmed salmon. Rest assured that if it does not say that the salmon is wild, it will be farmed and, until fishfarmers accept their responsibility to wildlife, we must refuse to take their product.

The recent virus which devastated the common seal stocks in 1988 further demonstrates how vulnerable seal populations are. Grey seals were also affected by the virus but to a lesser degree. However, the incidence of these epizootic disasters seems to be increasing with cases of mass mortalities in bottle-nosed dolphins, striped dolphins, harbour porpoises and Baikal seals – all this, as well as the phocine distemper virus, within the last five years.

Pollution levels are also increasing in our marine environment and these cause many problems including reduced fertility, birth deformities, uterine deformities, and the long-term effects are still largely unknown.

Then there are the deaths of countless marine animals including seals in drift nets, many of which float loose just collecting corpses as they go.

Grey seals face enough hazards as it is – predominantly man-made – and the suggestion of an official cull is therefore ridiculous. It is not even as though the grey seal is really common. In fact, it is one of the rarest seals in the world with a total population of only about 180,000 – that is less than half the number of elephants in the world and we are jumping up and down about them. Quite rightly so, of course, but if this is a dangerous level for elephants, why not for grey seals? To put this in another way, there are more people in Aberdeen than there are grey seals in the world. We just happen to be fortunate that we have a good percentage of them in British waters. And yet we seem to be happy to shirk our responsibility to give them the protection they deserve.

Under the Berne Convention, our government has a responsibility to protect both the common and grey seal. Seals are listed in Annexe III in this Convention, which states that they are protected animals, and the killing of them must be strictly licensed and controlled. Both the common and grey seal are also listed as species or animals threatened in the recent EEC Directive on the Protection of Natural Fauna and Flora in Europe. Our government continues to ignore these directives, but we will carry on our fight to give seals the protection they deserve, and we would ask you, the reader, to help us with this cause.

I suppose that, of all the members of the British wildlife heritage, no other creature has been more misunderstood than the fox, and over the years they have had a pretty bad press image. Foxes seem to be the scapegoat for much human hatred with regard to wildlife and while we are all horrified at the fate of this animal in areas where it is chased by a group of overweight geriatrics, many people think that all is safe in the Highlands. Nothing could be further from the truth.

The fox is one of our last remaining British carnivores, and it lives a largely nocturnal lifestyle, creeping around in the twilight zone, never really coming face to face with man if can avoid it. It is obviously a member of the dog family (the Canidae) and is a lot smaller than people imagine – roughly 90–130 centimetres long and about 8–14 kilograms in weight for an adult dog fox. However, its size is often exaggerated and we have heard frequent reports of foxes as big as golden retrievers taking fully grown rams!

I can remember one particular warm spring day at Suishnish, sitting beneath the crags at Carn Deag. All was quiet. A kestrel disappeared behind the hill to our left and we planned to walk on to the cleared village at Borreraig. Suddenly in front of us, a vixen appeared from behind a rocky outcrop. We stayed motionless. When you are watching wildlife, it is important to keep completely still but this is even more important with carnivores as they are conditioned to pick up movement of prey. Quite often you can watch for hours if you do not move. The vixen scurried onto the scree, her nose picking up scent from all around and she stared straight at us before moving away with a quick dart. Although we have observed foxes on many more occasions, to date this must be our finest sight of the animal. Her red-brown coat was in superb condition and glistened as the sun broke from behind a cloud.

Two weeks later the "fox controller" from the mainland did his rounds and the vixen was dead.

Around £70,000 per annum is spent through fox destruction clubs designed specifically to control this "vermin" of the countryside. Even the Forestry Commission – or Forest Enterprise, as it is now called – kill foxes as a so-called "good neighbours policy" to keep the local farmers and crofters happy, and they alone are responsible for the deaths of some 2000 adults and 800 cubs annually.

Farmers and crofters with the help of these so-called experts regularly blitz the fox and, in one area on the mainland, they wiped out all foxes within a five-mile radius of their village, only to find out that the sheep were still dying at the same rate as before.

In releasing our annual report one year, we highlighted this killing of foxes and it seemed to hit a raw nerve with one of our local crofters. We had had the tenancy of our croft for some five years then. It had started off as an area of three and a half acres of poor ground which had not been worked since about 1947, and after much effort in fencing, draining and reseeding it had started to look pretty good. We managed to get a job lot of Jacobs sheep which were joined by two Shetland sheep acquired from a friend. They had been with the tup over the winter and in May produced three lovely lambs – one small ewe and two ram lambs, but it was one of the ram lambs and the fox which was going to cause the trouble.

One of these blighters was a dedicated escape artist and, no matter how much we tried, it always managed to get through the fence into one croft, then through the next fence and into another field. This just happened to coincide with our press release on foxes. Mr Mcintyre, the neighbouring crofter, was not amused with the lamb. "Get this bloody sheep out of my land," he bellowed.

It took us about half an hour to bring the lamb back after chasing him around the croft, through the field, over the common grazing and back into our field. With a sigh of relief, we finished and made our way home for a well-deserved cup of tea.

The next morning the phone rang. Grace had already left in the minibus with a group of people and I was tidying up in the house with Kirsty and Ben, who was then two years old, for company. I picked up the phone and a loud voice yelled down the line. It was Mr MacIntyre. "Paul, your sheep is in our field eating my conifer trees. Get it out now." The phone slammed down.

Hurrying is difficult with two young children. I put Ben's coat and shoes on, got Kirsty ready on her bicycle, and placed Ben on the carrier of mine, only to discover that he had dirtied his nappy. Coat off, clothes off, nappy off, nappy on, clothes on, shoes on and coat on. Back on bicycle and eventually we were away.

We arrived at the croft and I left the two children playing on the grass. I walked up the croft to see a single figure striding towards me. He was walking with a sense of urgency, his face was twisted with rage. "I've warned you," he said. "Next time, I'll let the bloody thing out on the hill and let those foxes you are so friendly with deal with it." This is when I realised the true reason for his hatred towards me. Up until now, he had been generally friendly but for the last month this had changed and I could not for the life of me think that it was to do with that pesty lamb. Now I realised it was all to do with our campaign for the fox: he was one of those ardent fox-haters. He stomped off in such a temper that mud splattered on the back of his trousers and coat.

I stood there looking at the lamb, thinking how stupid sheep are. Why make all the effort to squeeze through a fence into another person's land when you have plenty to eat right here? But sheep are like that. Let's be truthful – anyone who has ever had sheep must realise that they are stupid, senseless individuals who are destined to do the most bizarre things in life. A sheep will venture down a sheer cliff face to eat one morsel of grass without a hope of being able to return back up the cliff to the pasture. A sheep will rush out in front a moving projectile (a car) without any warning and the faster the projectile moves the more likely the animal is to rush out in front of it. A group of sheep randomly placed in a field will round themselves up when approached within half a mile by an animal with four legs and a tail; the more black and white on that animal the faster the sheep will round up, and this is usually followed by the sheep frantically dashing across the field. Anyway, I must not dwell on sheep as it is the poor fox I want to consider.

Now I am not a particular expert on the effects of fox attacks on sheep as my knowledge come essentially from observing them in the field, but there are a number of scientific papers written on the subject. One study was commissioned by the League Against Cruel Sports and revealed that only about 0.5 to 1% of lambs are taken by the fox as compared with 24% of lambs lost to malnutrition, hypothermia, disease and stillbirths. To take another example, on the island of Mull there are no foxes and yet they lose the same number of lambs as areas on the mainland where there are healthy fox populations. Over the years, many local crofters have told us that they have no trouble with foxes on their land. Indeed, recently one lady told me that she had been sheep farming for 20 years and had only ever lost one weak lamb to a fox, in spite of the fact that she knew for certain that a family of foxes live in and amongst her flock.

If farmers actually looked after their sheep better and fenced them in from the roads, it would be a far more efficient way of using resources than spending all this time and money killing foxes. But then, as human beings, don't we often need someone or something else to blame?

After that encounter with Mr MacIntyre, we decided for diplomatic reasons to move the sheep down to the field next to the Centre. This is achieved not by a snapping collie dog. No, we go in for a far more efficient method than that, although I doubt we would win a prize at the local show. We round our sheep up using a combination of family power and food.

So one afternoon, we positioned our two children strategically at the two corners of the bottom field. Ben stood sucking his thumb while Kirsty waited eagerly with a stick. Now we were ready and all we needed was split second timing. I ran to the top of the field and started to move them down, while Grace ran along the far fence making sure they wouldn't bolt. Suddenly one of the sheep ran to the left followed by the rest and Grace quickly ran with tremendous precision cutting off the bolting sheep. Ben at the bottom of the field still stood with his thumb in his mouth. The sheep walked forward towards the gate and Grace ran round with her bowl of food. The first stage was over – now to move them down the road.

Sheep are incredibly greedy beasts, so Grace held a bowl of food in one hand and coaxed them on. We had done this many times, walking down the road with five sheep following and nothing had ever gone wrong. Mind you, on certain occasions it can be very embarrassing when we are confronted by foreign tourists who want to take pictures of these quaint Highland customs.

Eventually we moved all the sheep from the croft and proceeded down the lane and onto the road. Grace went ahead with the food bowl and I kept the rear guard with Kirsty and Ben.

Just as we reached Mr MacIntyre's driveway a car screeched around the corner and the sheep shot up his drive and started munching his flowers and lawn. I shouted at Grace to move around and she hurried into the garden trying desperately to get the sheep out and back onto the road. This proved to be more difficult than we would have thought as they seemed determined to reek as much havoc as possible, but after much shouting and waving of arms, we moved the animals out and back onto the road. Since then the sheep have not managed to escape from the croft again, although only time will tell if we are to have another Houdini character.

The problem with wildlife protection is that no matter how long or hard you try, you will never change the way certain people think. Some people will never be convinced that the fox has as much of a right to live as the over-subsidised sheep, and the same is true of other species. I was once talking to a salmon farmer from Shetland and he said to me in a serious manner "Why do we need seals? What good are they? If they all disappeared, the world would be a better place." With a mind as closed as that, there really is nothing you can do.

We believe that if we are to have any hope of protecting wildlife in the future, it is the children with their open and caring minds who are important, and we should be helping them to grow up with a love and respect for our natural environment.

Chapter 14 ~ Grace

"WHILE WE ARE BORN WITH CURIOSITY AND WONDER AND OUR EARLY YEARS FULL OF THE ADVENTURE THEY BRING, I KNOW SUCH INHERENT JOYS ARE OFTEN LOST. I ALSO KNOW THAT, BEING DEEP WITHIN US, THEIR LATENT GLOW CAN BE FANNED TO FLAME AGAIN BY AWARENESS AND AN OPEN MIND."

—SIGURD OLSEN

We teach our children to read and write, to learn about different countries, and yet we do not teach them how to live lightly on the planet. As parents, we all want the best for our children, and yet the ethos of our way of life today is undermining the very root of the life-support system upon which our own survival depends.

If you ask ten different people what they think is meant by "environmental education", you will receive ten different answers; ask ten different teachers what it means and your answers will be even more varied. I can remember talking to the local Boys Brigade one evening, and I held up a leaf and asked, "What is this?" "A leaf", one boy replied quite correctly. I delved further and asked, "But what does it do?" Back came the replies: "It grows on trees"; "It falls off in the autumn"; "It makes the trees look pretty."

These answers showed how we can recognise and maybe put names on things but we do not fully understand what they are, their role in the system of life and their true importance. It is a sad fact, and probably the result of the failure of our education system to teach what is really important, that not one of those twelve boys came even close to comprehend what a leaf really does: the fact that it and other green plants actually fix sunlight energy and give us oxygen, and these are the only things on our planet which can do this. And that oxygen itself is such wonderful stuff: sets the chemical potential of the planet, making it possible for engines to run, for eagles to fly and for us to live.

Today the concept of environmental education has been all but lost. Our life-support systems have come to mean nicely packaged food and drink, the automobile and a host of other gadgets. We have lost touch with the planet, and our world slips downhill: what a price we are paying for this materialistic progress! While the West basks in the shadow of prosperity, nearly three-quarters of the world's human population scrapes out an existence below the United Nations' world poverty level.

But we are not pessimists. We believe strongly that change will occur through our children, and we have to work closer and closer to these ideals with the children to teach them how to grow up with a respect and understanding of their natural environment. Real change comes only from the heart.

Working with children can be very tiring but it is so rewarding. They give so much back and often they ask questions which you have never really considered and which are crucial to real understanding. Never underestimate the thoughts of a child – they can be very deep. Children often ponder and ponder and then come out with a comment which puts many adults to shame.

We organise and run a local wildlife club and have developed an environmental prize in the Highlands and Islands area called quite fittingly the Seal of Approval. Children think very deeply; fundamentally they care because they have yet not been influenced by the forces of greed.

If I may, I would like to leave the rest of this chapter to the children and reproduce just a selection of the work from competitions we have organised over the years.

Below is a selection from Elgol School on Skye, who undertook an environmental assessment of their local seashore and were worried about all the dead puffins washing up.

Charles Kennedy MP
House of Commons

Dear Mr Kennedy

We are pupils from Elgol Primary School. The school is situated on the shoreline which is facing Soay and the Cuillins. We are involved in an environmental project, studying the shoreline in front of our school.

Before the end of last school term we were walking on the shore with our art teacher and we found 5 dead puffins on the high tide mark. We suspect that they died of starvation. Puffins are not usually found here dead or alive so they must have left somewhere else in search of food. Is there anything you can do to prevent the overfishing of sand eels because we are increasingly concerned and saddened by their plight?

Yours sincerely

Andrew Pickering (Aged 7)

THE PUFFIN

The Puffin is a lovely bird
Some people think it looks absurd
The only ones I've seen are dead
I wish I'd seen one live instead

WHERE ARE ALL MY FRIENDS GONE?

Puffins are gliding over the sea
Sandeels are sliding on the sand you see
Puffins are diving into the sea
Then one day man comes catching the eels
Puffins sit wondering
Can't find sand eels
The puffins are dying on our shore
And we sit crying on our shore
I'm angry, I'm sad
The beautiful birds are dying we had.

The following is a selection from Kyleakin Primary School who undertook a litter project.

CIGARETTE ENDS

Cigarette ends go away
Why stay and be untidy?
Go in the bin go in the fire
It's not your fault you are dangerous to animals
You're so untidy, don't want you
Your smoke gets in my eyes
You give people cancer
You destroy the environment

—*Darren*

THE GLASS BOTTLE

Smashed bottle
Might kill animals
And cut feet
Stupidly thrown away
Harmful in the countryside
Empty and useless, dangerous
Broken glass on the ground
Terrible people
They don't care
Let's stop them
Endangering the earth

—*Keith Mackenzie (Primary 7)*

Plockton Primary School entered a project on the Midge one year.

WHERE DO ALL THE MIDGES LIVE?

Where do the midges live, I ask
I'd kill myself to know
After they attacked us all
Where do they all go?

They don't live in the dustbin
They don't live in a nest
I asked a scientist where they lived
But he wouldn't tell me. Pest.

So I tried to find out for myself
By studying the land
But all I got out of that
Were stitches in my hand

One night I woke up with a jump
Something was tickling my head
And my legs and arms and feet
Ah, the midges home was in my bed.

—*Jane Mackinnon*

METHODS USED TO COMBAT THE DEADLY MIDGE

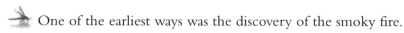

- One of the earliest ways was the discovery of the smoky fire.

- A pipe full of tobacco was used by fishermen in the nineteenth century.

- The common plant mugwort was recommended in the sixteenth century.

- By the 1920s several anti-midge recipes had been published using oils from various plants including lavender, lemon, lemon-grass, fleablane, wormwood, geranium, bitter orange, white cedar, cypress, eucalyptus, dill, fennel, juniper.

- The wearing of bright colours is thought to keep midges away as they are attracted to dark colours.

- In 1944, the Secretary of State for Scotland asked his scientific advisers to find out if there was a suitable chemical repellent available which could be used against midges. The repellent D.M.P was developed.

- In the late 1940s a second repellent appeared and D.E.E.T was developed. D.M.P and D.E.E.T still form the basis of most midge repellent today.

- The products produced which are based on these chemicals include Autan, Boots repellent, Jungle Formula, Mijex, Secto-Combat, Shoo, Deepwoods Off, Repel, Cutter, Muskol, Space Shield.

- The wearing of nets or nylon stockings on the head.

- Stay indoors.

Chapter 15 ~ Paul

"IN GOD'S WILDERNESS LIES THE HOPE OF THE WORLD —THE GREAT, FRESH, UNBLIGHTED,
UNREDEEMED WILDERNESS. THE GALLING HARNESS OF CIVILISATION DROPS OFF
AND THE WOUNDS HEAL 'ERE WE ARE AWARE"

—JOHN MUIR

Since its early beginnings, our charity has developed into one of the leading conservation bodies in the Highlands of Scotland. We not only work in Britain but are also developing a series of holidays to Switzerland and Russia and are working with conservation colleagues in these and other countries. Our Russian trip is designed specifically to look at some of the last remaining large populations of European mammal fauna, and when I visited over a year ago, it was like stepping back in time to what Scotland would have been like in times gone by.

Wild boar, elk, beaver, brown bear and, of course, Canis lupus – the grey wolf — roamed free around the forests of Scotland. When you are standing in the great Russian Taiga, it is hard to imagine that this forest once formed a band stretching right across the temperate regions of the Old and New World, and maybe here you are getting just a feel of what Scotland might have been like a thousand years ago, before we started destroying our forests.

When we look at the desolation of our Scottish hillsides at the present day, it hardly seems possible that at one time northern Scotland had this same habitat of forest and moorland, wild meadow, swamp and lake environments, together with a great variety of fauna – red deer, roe deer, elk and woodland caribou, typical rodents like red squirrel and beaver, and the larger predatory mammals like the brown bear, lynx, wildcat, fox, pine martin, stoat, weasel, European mink, otter, badger and of course the grey wolf.

A look at what fauna and flora remain and what has become extinct shows that our prehistoric wildlife in Scotland was mainly a forest fauna comparable with what I saw in

Russia. Whilst it cannot be argued that the destruction of our Scottish forests can be totally linked to human activity, as climatic effects also played a part, humans undoubtedly tipped the balance and took the reins of progress away from natural forces. Scottish forests have long since gone, whilst in Brazil today the Westerner dictates the destruction of the rainforests.

The way the land has been used since the destruction of these forests has had a dire effect on the fauna, but some people have suggested that it was the very fauna itself which was responsible for the forest destruction, bringing the argument full circle.

The wolf, for example, was one of the most harassed animals in this early Scotland. Many methods were employed for its control. In the eleventh century, during the reign of King Alexander, most wild creatures were reserved for the royal chase but no one was forbidden to hunt for the wolf. Indeed, bounties were put on their heads, and on 24 October 1491, the Treasury of Scotland paid five shillings to a man who brought two wolf heads to King James IV from Linlithgow.

In 1529 and 1530, Queen Mary witnessed the destruction of many wolves in royal hunts at Atholl. Yet despite all this, the wolf still survived to such an extent that some accounts describe the great pine woods of Rannoch and Lochaber as being impassable because of the wolves. Safe houses or spittals were erected if travellers were caught out by fading light and the Spittal of Glenshee in Perthshire is just one example of these. And yet there is no actual proof of anyone actually being killed by a wolf.

The wolf always managed to outsmart man until man started directly affecting its habitat. The ancient forests were cut down and burned, and the wolves in them, along with many other species, disappeared. By the end of the eighteenth century, the wolf was extinct in Scotland and with it had gone much of its forest.

But the wolf still outlasted some of Scotland's other mammal fauna: the lynx roamed in Neolithic times but man in defense of his flocks exterminated him long ago. How many of us could imagine brown bear roaming the forests of Scotland? Yet they were once found over the land from Dumfriesshire to Sutherland. A bear skull was found at Shaws and the canine tooth of a brown bear was discovered at Inchnadamph. The bear still survived in Scotland after the Romans had left and in Gaelic tradition there is the *Magh-Ghamhainn* – the paw calf, a rough dark grizzly monster. It appears that we eventually exterminated the bear along with the wild boar in the fifteenth century. The elk went out during the destruction of the forests and through hunting. The beaver lasted until about the fifteenth century before human activity again caused its extinction.

But in parts of Russia we still have this amazing forest with its rich fauna and flora spreading out for thousands of kilometres. My reason for visiting this land was to collaborate with Russian wildlife experts to establish one or two small ecological tourism schemes and our choice of the southern Taiga forest was because of its abundance of large European mammals. The region is run by the Central Forest State Reserve, which was set up by UNESCO as a Biosphere Research Station in 1947.

The reserve occupies an important ecological niche, the watershed for many of Russia's larger rivers – the Volga, Dneiper and Daugaua start here and empty their contents many hundreds of kilometres further on in the Black, Caspian and Baltic seas respectively.

Our wildlife trips to this area are designed not only to show people some of the last remaining populations of European large mammal fauna, but to counteract the threat of hunting in these more remote areas.

Already in parts of Russia, the hunting problem is increasing as big-time game hunters turn to the former USSR with it rich wildlife as prey for their guns. If we want to preserve this last unspoilt wilderness, it can be achieved by the right sort of tourism. People can live and the animals can be preserved for the future of the planet.

I did encounter wolves on this my first visit to Russia, and although on this occasion it was brief, it was exhilarating. In my short trip to the reserve, we did not see bear or elk, but our guides informed me that, given a little more time, this is possible.

On returning to Scotland, I was sitting on a train on the way to Kyle of Lochalsh. The hills and mountains looked bare and treeless, and it can be argued that these hillsides and glens, burns and lochs are not wild areas at all. Today they stand as unpopulated barren landscapes, a far cry from how they would have looked if only we still had the wolf.

But we do not appear to have learned at the present day. We still destroy wildlife in the name of sport, and persecute particularly our carnivores at an alarming rate. The fox is killed for just being a fox; otters, although legally protected, are also killed in certain areas; weasels and stoats are routinely slaughtered; and wildcats – well, being a carnivore, they must present a threat, so they too must die – and so the story goes on.

So what does the future hold for our wildlife? Being optimists, we have to be positive in our attitude and ensure not only that the animals survive but also that there is still a suitable environment for them. There is no point in working to preserve and restore habitat if all the natural inhabitants have gone. We have to ensure that we leave a legacy worth having for our children to inherit.

Today we share our home on Skye with our three children, Kirsty aged ten, Ben aged five and Connaire aged two. The children are involved in all our work from the beginning and they all love to help with the animals. Having children of our own makes it obvious to us that children have and will play more of an important role in our lives. As I write now, Ben and Kirsty are at school in Broadford and Connaire is asleep on the floor by my feet.

People sometimes ask how we manage to do things with the children. But that is just it – you do them *with* the children. They love nothing better than to come out and help feed and sort out the animals, and they have a far more realistic approach to death than I had as they have met it whenever we have lost a casualty. In fact, I am not afraid to say that Kirsty, at ten years of age, is still a lot better at coping with losing animals than I am now, and when we lost our old collie dog, she was comforting us and not the other way round.

Working with the animals with the children teaches them far more than books about so many things. They obviously learn which species is which; they learn what it eats; and – a very important lesson – which ones bite. They also find out at an early age the damage humans can inflict on wildlife and their habitat.

I consider our children very fortunate. How many others have had the opportunity to see seals, otters, and so many different birds at such close quarters without having to go to a zoo? I am not joking when I say that Ben's first word after the usual "Mummy" and "Daddy" was "Seal" and Connaire's was "Otter" and as far as Connaire was concerned every animal was an "Otter" (friends used to be in hysterics as he pointed at dogs, cats, everything and said enthusiastically "Otter".) This is because at the time when he was just starting to talk, we had two otter cubs in the hospital and so it just made sense to him.

Our children have also had the opportunity to visit some wonderful places and they come with us when we go in the winter on a "recky" for some new holiday trip. As yet, they are all too young to go to St Kilda, but soon they will be able to come and experience these wonderful islands too.

We hope our children will have a more realistic approach to life which will lead them to care for all that is around them. Like any parents, we often wonder what they will grow up to do. Of course, we would love them to continue the work of the Centre but we will support them all the way in whichever line they follow. The exact details of the profession they choose are not as important as the type of people they are; hopefully, we will have given them the opportunity to develop into caring people who are deeply concerned about the environment and all wildlife.

That our children do so is vital to us all.

Echoes of Camusfearna... The Video

The west of Scotland, one of the last strong-holds of the wild sea otter, was made famous by Gavin Maxwell and *Ring of Bright Water*. Today his legacy continues, through the work of Paul and Grace Yoxon, founders of the International Otter Survival Fund (IOSF). This film, with its haunting images of Camusfearna and Skye tells their story, and contains previously unseen footage of Gavin Maxwell with the otters.

Introduced and narrated by
Virginia McKenna

Star of *Ring of Bright Water* and *Born Free* and co-founder
of the Born Free Foundation

Photographed and directed by Joe Phillips. Written by Joe Phillips and Jeff Baron
Running Time 30 minutes approx • BHE 047 Echoes of Camusfearna £8.99

A Word About the IOSF...

The International Otter Survival Fund was set up not just to protect the Eurasian otter but to protect all 13 species of otter worldwide.

A world without these furry aquatic creatures would be a sad world – one without clean coastal waters, without clean river systems, lakes and estuaries. IOSF is working with people worldwide to identify threats to otters and taking steps to overcome these, and thus preserve some of the world's great habitats.

If you would like to help by becoming a member of IOSF, or by making a donation, please contact us at:

International Otter Survival Fund
Broadford
Isle of Skye
IV49 9AQ
Tel/Fax 01471 822487
email IOSF@aol.com
(Reg. Charity No. SC003875)

IOSF
INTERNATIONAL OTTER SURVIVAL FUND

BORN FREE The **Born Free Foundation** operates in many countries around the world trying to conserve wildlife and natural habitats. You can support this work or adopt animals in need of help by calling BFF on 01306 713320.

(Reg. Charity No. 296024)

Findhorn Press

is the publishing business of the Findhorn Community which has grown around the Findhorn Foundation, co-founded in 1962 by Peter and Eileen Caddy and Dorothy Maclean. The first books originated from the early interest in Eileen's guidance over 25 years ago and Findhorn Press now publishes not only Eileen Caddy's books of guidance and inspirational material, but also many others. It has also forged links with a number of like-minded authors and organisations.

For further information about the Findhorn Community and how to participate in its programmes, please write to:

The Accommodation Secretary
Findhorn Foundation
Cluny Hill College
Forres IV36 0RD, Scotland

Tel. +44 (0)1309 673655 Fax +44 (0)1309 673113
e-mail: reception@findhorn.org
http://www.gaia.org/findhorn/index.html/

For a complete catalogue or more information about Findhorn Press products, please contact:

Findhorn Press
The Park, Findhorn, Forres IV36 0TZ, Scotland
Tel. +44 (0)1309 690582 Fax +44 (0)1309 690036
e-mail: thierry@findhorn.org
http://www.gaia.org/findhornpress/